Whitehall

or

The days of George IV

Edited by

William Maginn

1827

PREFACE.

This singular work was printed in Teyo-
ninhakawaranenopolis, capital of the great empire of Yankeedoodoolia, in the year 2227,
exactly four hundred years from the present
date. The name of the author I do not know.
How it came into my hands, it were useless to
divulge; but I think it will be found to give
as graphic and correct a picture of the affairs
of the present day, as the general current of
our London historical novels give of the events

of four hundred years ago, when they treat of them.

I have nothing further to add, except that I have taken all proper care to puff the book, and hope it will be successful.

THE EDITOR.

N.B. Mr. Power, of the Strand, is the only person authorised to sell the poetry of this work, adapted to music.

Ed.

137, Oxford-Street.

WHITEHALL;

OR,

GEORGE IV.

CHAPTER I.

The historian commands attention, and rewards it, by selecting the more brilliant circumstances of great events, by unfolding the characteristic qualities of eminent personages, and by tracing well-known effects through all the obliquities, and all the recesses of their secret causes.

PARR.

IT was about five o'clock of the afternoon of Sunday, April the first, in the twenty-seventh year of the nineteenth century, when George IV. was King of England, that the Dover mail-coach, called (in compliment to one of the most eminent statesmen of that time), *the El-don,* approached, with that velocity for which its movements, like those of its namesake, were ever distinguished, the magnificent bridge of

Westminster, then forming one of the most popular as well as splendid approaches to the overgrown and luxurious metropolis of the Britannic empire. Two of the persons seated on the summit of the vehicle, were observed by the multitude of on-.ookers to contemplate the scene before tnem with the intense and fixed gaze of surprise and wonder. It was obvious to the most superficial glance that they had never seen London before. Their demeanour was now studied with increasing anxiety, and a murmur of inquiry began to be diffused among the multitudinous mass :—" Who," said many a startled citizen, " are these stedfast starers? From what far distant region have they been wafted to the shores of free and happy England ?"

" I am decidedly of opinion," remarked a strong-built man of middle age to his wife (who, according to the interesting manners of the period, had her arm linked in his)—" I am decidedly of opinion that this is a young nabob from the East Indies. The great Chinese fleet has, according to the *John Bull** of this morning, arrived safely in the Channel.'

" Methinks," replied the lady, " the broad-brimmed hat of white straw, which forms part of his costume, points rather to a western than to an eastern origin. Depend upon it, my love, 'tis a planter from Jamaica."

" I hope so," returned the husband, " for we have been anxiously looking for ships from that quarter. Limes are extremely scarce, dear, and (I must say) bad at this moment; and those black devils appear to be in a pretty state—rot them. I dined, as you are aware, yesterday, at the Thatched House, and positively the punch for the turtle was made with lemons alone——"

* *John Bull.* The principal church and monarchy news-paper of the time, and written by the most learned members of the hierarchy. The jocose papers—afterwards gathered in a volume, and published by John Murray in 1830—were chiefly the productions of Bothers, Bishop of Norwich.

" Bless us !" said the affectionate dame—
" not a single lime at the Thatched House !"

This conversation took place during the time
that the guard and coachman of the Eldon were
enjoying a cup of Lamb's-wool (*i. e.* lukewarm
milk and rum), opposite the gates of the Elephant
and Castle hostelrie ; the last pause which was
to occur in the course of their present journey.
The closing drop of the nutritive and exhilarating
beverage had now been imbibed ; the vessels
had been returned into the hands of the smiling
Boniface ; * the conductor received once more
into his own skilful fingers the reins, which had
been entrusted for the moment to a stern-looking
passenger in a huge military cloak of blue
cloth, trimmed luxuriously with ermine and
scarlet, a bear-skin foraging cap, St. Albans,†

---

* Boniface, *i. e.* Innkeeper. *Vide* the Rev. Dr. Toddy's
edition of Johnson.

† St. Albans. The name of a fashionable species of
breeches, so called after the Duke of St. Albans, Master
of the Ordnance to George IV.

and Wellingtons; * the guard, lifting his resplendent horn to his lips, sounded the first
movement of the *Rule Britannia*, and in a second
the foaming horses were again in full career for
Regent-street.

" Well, off they go," cries the lady; " we
shall see what the newspapers have got to say in
the morning; but, on second thoughts, my dear,
I'll lay my life that that there youth on the near
side, though he has a black with him, is no more
a West Indian than I am."

" What do you mean ?" said Hawkins.

" I mean that he looks like a gentleman," was
the reply.

" And are there no gentlemen in the West
Indies ?" retorted Hawkins. " I'm sure, there
was Major Fellowes, that you knew at Worthing
—did *you* think the Major was not a gentleman,
Ma'am ?"

---

* Wellingtons, *i. e.* military top-boots, named after the
celebrated general who introduced and patronized them.

" They told us he had a wonderful fine property in Demerara," was the apparently indifferent reply.

" A fine property, indeed !" sneered the
gentleman ; " a property chiefly of human flesh,
I believe, as you call it. But why should we
fall out about this Johnny Newcome ? 'Tis no
concern of ours—is it, Lucy, my darling ?"

The last words were addressed to a young
female, who had taken no part in this conversation, and her only answer was a start and a long-
drawn sigh.

" What's the matter, my love ?" says the
father ; " you look very pale, Lucy—what has
come over thee, girl ?"

Still no answer.

" Oh ! nonsense," said the elder female ;
" there's nothing wrong with Lucy, but what
her dinner will set to rights. Come, let's be
moving. The mutton will be roasted to rags
ere we can reach Portland-place."

The poor girl grasped her father's arm, and
the party proceeded on their way for some time
in total silence. They had reached the centre
of the bridge when Mrs. Hawkins (for that was
the name of the family) jogged Mr. Hawkins
on the elbow, and asked, in a hurried tone,
" who was that lady that bowed to you from
the green *barouche* ?"*

" That lady," replied Hawkins, with a sim-
per—" why that lady is Madame Vestris."†

" And how do you know any thing of Madame Vestris, Mr. Hawkins ?"—and Mrs. Hawkins fanned herself.

" I met her down in Gloucestershire last
Christmas," he answered—" she is a charming
actress; French, English, Italian, all come alike
to her. Really a wonderful creature."

" Mr. Hawkins," said the lady, " there's no

* Barouche. It is now the generally received opinion
that this vehicle was a low phaeton with four wheels. See,
however, Bacon Sangareeville, vol. iii. p. 505, and the
references of the Appendix.

understanding you—there again! another nod!
Upon my word, you have no scarcity of acquaintance."

" I never saw Lady Caroline looking better,"
ejaculated Hawkins—" quite in bloom, 'pon
my honour. Lucy, my dear," he continued,
" what sets thee a shivering and shaking so ?—
I protest thou art affected with some malady
that should be seen to."

" O, no, Sir" sighed Lucy—" there's nothing in the world the matter with me."

" I believe not, indeed," replied Mrs. Hawkins the second. " Bless us, there's the Dover
coach again. My eye, she's setting down all
her passengers at Holmes's."

" And a very comfortable hotel it is," says
Hawkins—" our friend with the white hat has
made a very good election. Only look what a
quantity of luggage they are getting out of the
boot."*

* Boot. See Transactions of the Kentucky Royal So-

" By this time the party had reached the entrance of Holmes's hotel. Several passengers stood on the pavement superintending the delivery of their baggage. An elderly African, of a noble corpulence, and shewing all his fine teeth, in a smile of exquisite delight, was among the rest receiving sundry portmanteaus, *sacs-de-nuit*, trunks, dressing cases, hat-boxes, &c. &c. &c. from the guard of the Eldon; and three sharp-eyed, nimbled-jointed aids or waiters were assisting him. The unknown, who had struck Mrs. Hawkins as having the air of a gentleman, said, just as the pedestrians were passing him—" Cæsar, mind my shaving things;" when he was interrupted by a short, quick, piercing scream. Lucy Hawkins gasped for breath, staggered, and fainted. The stranger rushed forwards, caught the beautiful creature in his arms; and, motioning to Hawkins, bore her, without the delay of a moment, into the hotel.

The crowd which had been attracted and

detained by these occurrences, soon dispersed,
and the Eldon drove off with redoubled speed.
On more than one observer, however, a considerable impression had been made; and the
singular grace and elegance of the unknown
maiden's figure and features continued to form
a common topic of consideration during several
ensuing hours. The Speaker of the House of
Commons, dressed in his full official costume,
happened to have been passing at the moment
when Lucy swooned away in the arms of the
interesting stranger, (who, we may remark, *par
parenthese*, was decidedly a Creole) in company
with the Right Honourable Henry Brougham,
Sir Daniel Whittle Harvey,* the Marquis of
Londonderry, and some other eminent statesmen of the times; and this distinguished party
separated almost immediately afterwards; the
Marquis turning down Downing Street, where

* Afterwards Lord Keeper, under the title of Viscount
Whittleton, of Costschester.

he was engaged to an early family dinner party
with that too celebrated descendant of the martyred Byng—known by the fatal surname of
Poodle; while the Speaker and Sir Daniel continued their walk to Lambeth, and Brougham
seeing the venerable patriot Raikes pass along
alone in his cabriolet, took a seat by his side
and returned to Brookes's.* The consequence
was, that the intelligence of what had happened
was immediately conveyed into some of the
most influential circles in the capital. The
charms of the lovely unknown were discussed
with zealous interest by the assembled heads of
the opposition in their favourite rendezvous,
and a solemn bumper to her recovery was
among the earliest healths of that festive board.
Three cabinet ministers, who were that day
taking a quiet beef-steak and a cigar together at
the Foreign Office, to discuss an approaching

---

* Brookes's. A celebrated whig chop-house. (See the
Encyclopædia, *sub voce.*)

question of the first moment, were not less affected by the glowing narrative of the youthful,
yet veteran chieftain of the celebrated Tenth
Legion. Nor were Dr. Parr, Mr. Edward Irving, the Bishops of Chester and Gretna Green,
and the venerable Earls Harborough and Bexley,
who had dropt in to partake in the Lord Primate's celebrated pork-chops* and peach brandy,
at all insensible to the enthusiastic encomiums
in which the Speaker and his interesting friend,
Sir Daniel Whittle Harvey, strove to outvie each
other.

Lucy Hawkins was the heroine of the event-
ful evening.

* The antiquarian reader will be reminded of the song
in " Old English Ditties,"
" Lord Wenables eats turtles,
" Lord Primate, he eats Thurtells," &c. &c.
Vol. iii. p. 246.
Thurtells were pork-chops, so called, it is supposed,
from a butcher of Ware, who excelled in them. The
Reverend Dr. Toddy is quite wrong, as usual, on this
point.

CHAPTER II.

" I hope I don't intrude."

OLD PLAY.

" ENCHANTING girl !" said the unfortunate youth to himself, as soon as the hackney coach had borne from the door of the hotel, the im-perfectly recovered Lucy—" Enchanting girl! miserable man ! what hope can be for me ?—what link can ever connect the fortunes of this radiant angel and the desolate Smithers ?"

Cæsar entered the parlour some minutes after-wards, and found his master still sitting with one elbow on the sideboard, and holding in the other hand the tumbler which Lucy Hawkins had touched with her lips, and in which three or four tiny bubbles of the soda water yet lin-gered. The good old man with instinctive

discrimination, saw at once how deeply his
master had been affected—a kindred heart beat
beneath the dusky bosom of the tried dependant,
and forbearing from idle questions, his delicate
tact took upon itself the arrangement of every
detail. In a word, the dinner was ordered and
set silently upon the table, ere yet our hero
(for such in truth he is) had at all vanquished,
by the suggestions of reason, the morbid influence of that passionate stupor.

Minds of gigantic vigour, however, contain
within themselves an ever salutary principle of
elasticity, of whose intense energies vulgar souls
will in vain attempt to realize any adequate imagination: and so it was with Smithers upon
this trying emergence. Cæsar, motioning to the
waiter that his attendance might be dispensed
with, lifted, with his own hand, the cover from
a dish of the most beautiful herrings, and
another of mashed potatoes, and said in a cheer-
ful accent, "Come, Massa John." To have

said more would have been superfluous. The whole truth of his situation at once rushed into the mind of Smithers.—" Fool, driveller, that I am !" he muttered to himself, rising impetuously from the hair-bottomed chair which had so long detained him.—" Madman, idiot, recreant, traitor, poltroon ! Is it for this that I have sworn the deadly vow— ? Is it for this that I have abandoned the solitary matron ?— But hold—that word must not be uttered beneath a foreign sky—Is it for this that I tread the soil of England, that I breathe the atmosphere of the capital of George ?"—A smile of noble and elevated exultation passed over his lips, as he internally continued the strain of thought. " Is it for ends like these that I am actually within the same city with a Buxton, a Brougham, and a Wilberforce ?"—But a red light gleamed in his eyes as the glance of intellect shot on to the ideas of the tyrannic Liverpool and his instrument of ire, the ferocious Michael Angelo Taylor—

disgrace of that highborn and heroic name. In
this mood John Jeremy seated himself, and devoured with rapid earnestness the viands which
Cæsar had provided. Some boiled veal and
bacon and greens terminated the repast, during which the youth emptied two pots of delicious porter, doubly endeared to his palate by
its title of "Buxton's Entire;" and finally,
Cæsar putting a pint of Cape Madeira and a
noggin of rum on the table, retired to eat his
own dinner in an adjoining apartment, where, exhausted with fatigue, and tempted with new
liquors of the richest influence, he soon yielded
up his reason to the powers of intoxication.

Our hero thus left in solitude, began, sipping
insensibly the fluids before him, to ponder over
the particulars of his present situation and future
conduct, with that calm self-command which
formed one of the primary qualities of his
character, and to arrange and revise the letters
of introduction and other documents which had

been entrusted to his keeping. The result of his deliberations was, that as soon as another day had broken upon the world, he should proceed at once to seek out the distinguished philanthropist Zebediah Macfarlane, and lay before him in their utmost truth of detail the unparalleled circumstances under which he had torn, himself from the soil of his birth, and planted his foot upon that of his paternal ancestry. " Yes," said he to himself—" there can be no use for dilatory procrastination and imbecile hesitation *now*; I have set my fortunes upon a cast—I *will* go to-morrow, immediately after breakfast, to the immortal Macfarlane."

To finish what remained of his rum, to lock up his documents in a small portable case, to ring the bell and desire the attendance of the chambermaid, was the work of a moment.

Smithers was conducted to a neat bed-room, up three pair of stairs, by a comely damsel, who bore the candlestick before him with an air

of native grace, which redeemed within the
boundaries of respect the menial character of
her functions. Placing it on a little table covered
with a napkin of snowy whiteness, she cast her
fine grey eyes full upon him, and then dropping over them large and tender lids, which par-
took in the suffusion of rosy modesty that had
now mounted upwards from bosom, neck, and
cheek, said in a tone of tremulous gentleness,
" Missis don't allow no snuffers or 'stinguish-
ers; but if you ring when you are in bed, Sir, I
will come and fetch away the light."

" I respect the precaution," said Smithers,
" which dictated this regulation, and when I
ring you will find the candle outside the door."

The poor girl started and met Smithers' eye.
The blood recoiled from her visage; and pale
as a statue, trembling as a leaf, she turned
away from the pure and penetrating, but neither
haughty nor triumphant, glance of virtue. She
retreated in silence; and there was that about

her humbled demeanour which would not suffer him to repress a cordial "good night." The young woman thanked him by a melancholy, half-formed smile. No unworthy emotion of scorn or pride found even a momentary shelter within the breast of Smithers; but we see no reason why we should suppress the fact, that as he lay down, "severe in youthful beauty," and "naked in his innocence," a sweet vision seemed to pass lightly before him, and diffuse over his inmost heart-strings a breath of softening and soothing gratulation. "Angelic form," he inly whispered, "desert not the fancy when slumber folds her light wings over the gross world of reality. Be mine, Lucy, be mine, thou peerless loveliness, be mine at least in my dreams."

Oh! enviable elasticity of youth and hope! The destined participator in a thousand perils, the sworn avenger of blood-buried virtue, closed, ere many minutes elapsed, those eyes which she who had once perused their deep and

majestic mystery of sentiment could never forget, in sleep as calm as ever rested on the cradle
of an unconscious infant. . In vain was all the
hum of men, all the trampling of steeds, all the
rush and roar of carriages ; in vain did the
bugle and the trumpet speak and echo the sig-
nals of the night from tower to fort, and from
camp to barrack ; in vain did the sonorous peal-
ing of a thousand bells from chapel, church,
abbey, and cathedral, disturb the pillow of darkness; in vain did hoarse watchmen and horse-
patroles shout ever and anon the harsh announcement of the progressive march of time ;
in vain did arriving guests, in every stage of
inebriety, scream within the hotel itself for
waiters, chambermaids, candlesticks, warming-
pans, toast water, ginger beer, porter, negus,
bishop and grog ; in vain was the night broken
by clamours after punch, and the morning startled by cries for purl ; the whole turbulence and
hubbub of the nocturnal babel fell unheeded on

the dreaming ear, while the airy power of un-
fettered imagination had overleaped all barriers
and boundaries of space, circumstance, and law,
and pressed the lip of youthful constancy to the
cheek of far distant beauty.

CHAPTER III.

Can tyrants but by tyrants vanquished be,
And freedom find no champion and no child ?

BYRON.

IT was one of the old maxims of the genuine
unsophisticated wisdom of yet undegraded
England which proclaimed that

" Early to bed, and early to rise,
Is the way to be healthy, and wealthy, and wise;"

and in the spirit of this venerable saying, had
our young hero been trained up from his earliest
infancy by the saintly parent now entombed beneath the sod of an insulted land. That parent's
precepts, however, had survived in all their

strength of influence the savage blow that levelled
his existence with the dust; and the first-born
of his heart rung with determined hand for hot
water exactly at half past eight on Monday
morning, and before the authoritative clock of
the Horse-Guards' chapel* had struck the hour
of nine, he was already seated at one of the
numerous breakfast tables of the great or public
saloon of Holmes's hotel. The aids mentioned
in a tone of regretful concern, that owing to the
arrival of new company during the night, they
could no longer give him possession of the parlour he had occupied the preceding evening,
but that ere that day was over they should have
a better at his service. Little did they know of
Smithers, who could for a moment suspect him
of attaching any importance to such trivial
things as these. The young man replied with
a smile, the benignity of which at once restored

* See Vicomte de Marmalades Antiquités Militaires de
la Grande Bretagne, tom. 3. p. 543.

these vulgar spirits to tranquillity, that, " he
would as soon breakfast in the coffee-room as in
the proudest retirements of the establishment."

Having finished a slight and simple meal,
the youth now prepared for the business of the
day. The attention of the hotel-keeper soon
provided him with an experienced guide, under
whose direction the most intricate recesses of
the vast metropolis might be traversed with ease
and safety ; and dressed in weeds of the deepest
mourning, with a long crape round his white
straw-hat, Smithers sallied forth at once into
Parliament-street. The faithful Cæsar followed
him, bearing the documents, to which we have
already alluded, in a green bag under his left
arm, while a stout bamboo, carried with an air
of the most fearless determination over the right
shoulder, manifested the proud feelings with
which the emancipated bondsman was resolved
to protect the precious deposit with which he
found himself entrusted. The guide, by name

Peter Cheltenham, was a light active lad, the natural son of a proud noble who had never condescended to take the smallest care of his education, but abandoned him, with the most heartless indifference, to be tossed about like a vessel without helm or helmsman on the wide sea of life. It was, therefore, no wonder that he occupied the situation of runner, or message-bearer, in Mr. Holmes's employment; nor if, in the course of existence to which he thus from necessity submitted, he had acquired, together with an intimate knowledge of the streets, lanes, and squares of London, something also of unsettled character, a certain cynical contempt for the established forms of social intercourse, and a lamentable indifference to religious sanctions, ought the blame to be exclusively attached to the unfortunate stripling himself. Gay of heart, and airy of demeanour, Peter Cheltenham was one of those short-sighted individuals who establish it as their principal rule of conduct to

take things as they find them, and would re-
luctantly consider that day as ill spent in which
moderate exertion had been rewarded with the
means of making a comfortable dinner, and en-
oying a merry carouse after an equally satis-
factory supper, in company with some loose
minded, jolly, toping cad*, or under groom, or
perhaps some lovely but capricious and incon-
stant " cynthia of the minute." Such was our
hero's new attendant, the mere creature of circumstances, the very sport of fortune—: But
to our tale——

Cæsar did not perhaps regard with deeper
feelings of astonishment than his master the
scenes of novel splendour which developed themselves as the party ascended towards Whitehall,
and so on to the heart of the political region of
the British metropolis ; but the openness with
which his comparatively uncultivated mind revealed its impressions, afforded a signal contrast

* *Cad.* Vide Archdeacon Ignare's Glossary, *sub voce.*

to the quiet demeanour of Smithers. His eyes
now roamed about dazzled and distracted, now
rested with a basilisk stedfastness on some one
commanding object of wonder: and the reader
can hardly need to be told that such gestures as
these, accompanied as they were by many an
unsophisticated ejaculation, forcibly attracted
the notice, and amused the fancy of the practised
Cockney*, Peter. To confess the truth, Cheltenham early discovered a rich vein of merriment
in the simple African; nor was he slow to work
what he had thus detected. The rude ribaldry,
however, in which he began to indulge called
down ere long the grave and manly rebuke of
Smithers; and the lad, resolving to reserve Cæsar
for a private perambulation, proceeded to explain to our hero himself in a respectful manner
the several structures which appeared to excite
his admiration, pointing out occasionally, as
he went on, such eminent individuals as hap-

* *Cockney.* Vide Archdeacon Ignare's Glossary *sub voce.*

pened to pass them in that tumultuous thorough-
fare.

On one side of the way Cheltenham directed
the eye of Smithers to that superb establishment
in which the naval empire of England was then
administered. A gigantic Neptune, leaning on
his trident, in the midst of an enormous fountain
of marble, around whose edge thirty sea-horses
and dolphins spouted water in many a playful
circumgyration, seemed to guard the main access
to the princely edifice; while on either side a
long range of statues by Cibber, Flaxman,
Chantry, and Roubilliac recalled the glories of
the principal marine heroes of the state. Here,
for example, appeared the indomitable sturdiness
of a Blake, there the serene dignity of a Shovel:
on one hand an immense bronze steam-boat forms
an appropriate basis for the colossal height of
Cochrane, the emancipator of Greece, and the
conqueror of Egypt; while immediately opposite to him is seen the one-armed Nelson, writhing

Under the arrow of Fate, (who hovers in the
distance on the mimic mast of a hostile admiral,)
and supported between the weeping figures of
Magnanimity and Captain Hardy, Britannia, and
Lady Hamilton. Lost in a maze of agitating
reflections, Smithers and his African stood so
long before these miracles of art, that the group
at length attracted the observation of the Captain of Marines, who with his troop kept guard
on horseback in front of the naval palace; and
this gentleman, by name Parry, thought it his
duty to convey the suspicions which had been
excited in his mind to the authorities in the interior. The result may easily be guessed. At
that period the fermentation of popular sentiment in the Antillic Colonies was at its height,
and the alarming truth was but too well known
at the council-board of the Lord High Admiral
of England. " The case is plain;" said a mea-

---

* *Parry*. Subsequently discoverer of the North Pole,
and Governor of Barrowtaria.

gre, fiery-faced veteran, who occupied the seat at
the right hand of the president. " The news
of last night are but too fully confirmed! Barbadoes, Demerara, Jamaica herself, are on the
eve of insurrection! Let us have these creole
vagabonds before us without the delay of
another moment."

" Ah! Geordie Warrender," said the president, with a gentle smile, and tapping a huge
*mull** made out of the horn of a moose deer, and
garnished with a jingling appendage of chains,
brushes, spoons, &c.† " commend me to thee,
mon, for finding oot the sting o' a bumbee! I'se
warrant they're just e'en tway three idle land-
loupers gapin at the Leeons o' Lunnun. Hoot
away, mon, hoot away, wi ye noo. I mind
weel, my father, puir mon, tellin' us when we
were wee weans how he gapit, and glowrit aboot

* *Mull, &c.* Vide Professor Jamieson's Dictionary of the
Scottish Language.

† See Caledonia Antiqua, by Professor Schwamm,
Vol. 2. pp. 230. 276.

at a'thing, whan he came up a raw laddie,
wi' a towzy head and twal puns Scotch in his
poke, like the Eesralites to Canaan in quest o' a
land o' milk and honey."

"My Lord," replied Warrender firmly,
"your Excellency may laugh as long as you
please; but I must repeat my caution. My
lord, it is my duty to protest against this frigid
indifference at such a crisis as is here!" So saying, the old admiral rose from his place. Solemnly
laying his hand upon his breast, he cast his
fierce eye around the circle, and cried, with the
voice of a Stentor, " I charge you, gentlemen,
to do your duties as I have done mine." A stamp
with the wooden leg (which supplied the place
of that lost at La Hogue), gave additional
energy to the exclamation.

"Arrah now, sure Milvil, my frind," whispers
the secretary, " what's the fun of this? Is it
any harm to have up the pretty boys, and be
tipping them a little touch of the long pole?"

" Bring them in, bring them in," said several voices.

" Weel, weel," cries the Lord High Admiral; " my conscience! wullfu' bodies wull hae their ain gait ; he that will to Cupar, maun to Cupar." With this he nodded to the secretary, who instantly began to draw out the necessary warrants; but it was obvious how much the temperate chief still disapproved of the proceedings into which the tumult of a popular assembly was hurrying him. He said nothing, except " Havers, havers, a' havers, by Bannockburn !" in a whisper ; but he strode with passionate gestures towards the window, his tartans rustling vehemently, and the dirk and claymore ringing audibly with every movement of his martial frame.

The government of Britain, it may be well nigh superfluous to observe, though keeping up a certain external show of liberal institutions, habeas corpus, hustings, jury-trial, Houses of Parliament, unpaid magistrates, forty shilling

voters, common council assemblies, county meet-
ings, &c. &c., had long ere the time at which we
take up a portion of her history, degenerated in
reality into a practical despotism, but little less
offensive in its operation than the avowed auto-
cracies of St. Petersburgh or Byzantium. No
sooner, therefore, were the documents subscribed
and sealed, than Smithers, Cæsar and Cheltenham found themselves marching between double
files of dragoons toward the council-room of the
Admiralty. Hazardous as our hero could not
but feel his position to be, it was still impossible
for him to traverse the magnificent corridors of
this enormous pile without lending a momentary
tribute of attention to the gorgeous display
which they unfolded to the unaccustomed gaze.
A singularly noble and picturesque imagination
had presided over the conceptions of the archi-
tect who reared those unrivalled halls. The
roofs, whose altitude surpassed conjecture, were
painted so as to represent the heavens under

D

every possibility of storm and calm. Over one
saloon unnumbered stars of gold or silver gleamed
steadily on a firmament of the serenest azure.
In a second, a floating mass of clouds were
tinged with the richest hues of an autumnal sun-
set. In a third, the luminary of day broad and
scarlet was seen cleaving the cold mist of a De-
cember morn. In a fourth, a resplendent rainbow spanned with its magical arch the concave
of a recently troubled expanse. In a fifth, the
upturned eye shrunk instinctively from the fear-
fully veracious portraiture of lurid clouds and
flashing lightnings with which the whole canvas
seemed to be impregnated. The innumerable
banners won in a thousand sea-fights from the
enemies of England hung waving in the breeze
that coursed through the upper air of these
haughty saloons; the flag of Suetonius Paulinus
taken at Mona, floated here in unconscious con-
tact with that which Saladin's *Dromound* struck
to Cœur de Lion on the one hand, and the more

richly blazoned ensign which De Winter yielded
to Duncan on the other. Gigantic cartoons
of the most startling discoveries and terrific en-
gagements covered the upper walls: and ranged
along the ground some hundreds of stern-eyed
men-of-wars' men of every gradation of rank,
armed to the teeth with spears, blunderbusses,
boarding-pikes, hand-grenades, steam-guns, and
Congreve rockets, prescribed the assurance of a
power against which resistance must to the
boldest group of individuals, have been entirely
hopeless. Smithers passed on in silence, conscious of innocence and resigned to fate: Cæsar
utterly unable to comprehend the events of the
morning, followed him with a gaze of anxious
stupor, yet without the smallest appearance of
trembling. Cheltenham marched the last of the
three. He was not one of those who carry their
hearts upon their sleeves; yet it could not be
concealed that he felt the unpleasantness of his
situation, at least, as painfully as either of the

strangers who preceded him. Yet he was not
altogether unpractised in such scenes, and his
mind reverted to occurrences in Bow-street,
where he had borne a principal part, having by
the mild and virtuous Birnie been, after an ingenious defence, committed to that gyratory
mender of manners which revolved in the subur-
ban shades of Brixton.

The procession at length reached an inner
court of Saracenic architecture, in the midst of
which three cannons of the largest dimensions,
attended by a suitable party of artillery men
with matches ready lighted, announced the im-
mediate vicinity of the conclave.* Commodore
Parry, commanding the whole band to sound a
solemn note of warning, advanced within the
massive arcade, and knocking three times with
the hilt of his sabre upon the iron gates of the

* Marmalade's Antiquités Militaires, tom. 5. pp. 32,
87, 93, 164, 233.

council chamber, reported in the accustomed formula of words, that he had performed his duty, and that the prisoners were in attendance. A brief, but anxious pause ensued; and Sir George Naylor, in his heraldic scarf and tabard issuing from the portal, uttered, amidst the breathless silence of the expectant bystanders, the decisive words:—

" O yes, O yes, O yes! Be it known, that Donald, by the grace of God, Lord High Admiral of Great Britain, France and Ireland, herewithin present in council, commandeth the personal attendance forthwith of three men, names as yet unknown, now in the custody of his excellency's guard."

He added in a more familiar tone, " Commodore Parry will search the prisoners, deprive them of their arms and papers, &c. and conduct them into the presence of the board between three files of picked grenadiers."

The Commodore signed imperatively to a subaltern officer; and he in his turn nodded significantly to a serjeant of colossal stature, who, halbert in hand, stept forward to the sound of a solitary bugle. The prisoners offered no resistance; and the satellite of despotism began with a grin of savage exultation to ransack every part of their persons. Two penknives and Cæsar's bamboo were all, we need scarcely observe, that could be discovered in the shape of arms; but the addresses of the letters in the green bag, appeared to call up feelings of the liveliest description in the breasts of the inspectors. Little or nothing was said audibly; but a deep muttering and glances of ardent suspicion were sufficiently intelligible. After a momentary pause, Parry, gathering all the articles into the bag, moved once more towards the half open gate of entrance; and the victims of oppression followed with downcast eyes, each individual guarded between two soldiers with drawn faulchions, while the bugle to which we alluded above, marked with its agitated and wailing notes every step that they progressed.

CHAPTER IV.

Now's the day and now's the hour,
See the front of battle lour.

BRAHAM.

THE first hurried glance which Smithers cast around the council-room, shewed him a numerous company of dignified persons, chiefly in naval uniforms, many of them wearing the insignia of the Bath and Guelphic orders, seated around a large circular table covered with deep blue velvet, embroidered all over with anchors and naval crowns. The president, as has already been hinted, appeared in the noble garb of his clan at the upper end of the table; a gorgeous canopy of silk tartan, with thistle plumes waved

over his chair of state, and an enormous two
handed claymore half-drawn out of its crimson-
satin scabbard lay immediately before him, and
close to the mace and fasces which formed more
strictly speaking the proper ensigns of his
authority. Apart a little way, at a separate
table of smaller dimensions, sat the secretary of
state for the naval department, in a richly furred
gown of black velvet, and gold chain of *SS*.
He wore that singularly shaped mitre of yellow
corduroy decorated with bells, which was the
strange emblem of his office, while a bunch of
shamrocks at the button-hole of his inner vest,
and the pale blue cordon of St. Patrick,
announced, before he spoke a single word, that
a native of " Green Erin" could still occupy
this important office. *After* he spoke his country needed no other announcement. The apartment, it may be observed, though of magnificent
extent, was so framed and furnished as to present the complete likeness of a marine cabin. An

orrery of gigantic size swung from the centre of
the tent-like roof, the armour of renowned admi-
rals of the olden times decorated the walls, and
the grand banner of England hung in heavy
folds at the farther extremity of a saloon.   The
scene was imposing, nor had the circumstances
under which Smithers surveyed it any tendency
to diminish its natural impression.

The secretary received the green-bag, and
produced the letters, which it was voted by
acclamation should immediately be opened; and
while he was doing this, the president waving
one hand, while the other was busily occupied
in relieving a titillating sensation in his nether
extremity, addressed in a perfectly mild tone of
voice the prisoners at the bar,

"Weel, lads," said he; "the best gait for
a' concerned wull e'en be, that ye make a clean
breast o't, and tell us at ance wha ye are, whare
ye came frae, and what's your buzzness in Lunnun ?"

" John Jeremy Smithers !" interrupts the
secretary, who had just finished reading the
first document, " which is the poet among you
that answers to that ?"

" I do"—said our hero firmly, with a voice
that echoed through the vaulted roof.

" Nay, nay," interrupted the president, " the
cheeld need na say ony thing that may meeli-
tate against himsell gin he does na like.* Ye'll
mind the case of my father, puir mon, and that
body Trotter."

" I understand your meaning, my lord,"
cries Smithers, " and I thank you for your
compasionate consideration of an unfortunate
stranger's case : but come weal, come woe, I
scorn to retract the admission which has once
proceeded from my lips. Let who will take
refuge under the shelter of cold and barren
forms, far be from me and mine the heart that

* Vide Blackstone, Vol. II. p. 333.

could brook such degradation. Here I am, a free born, and an innocent man—let power look to . its own proceedings—I rely solely on the strength of that guardian so beautifully mentioned in the page of Dante—yes, my lords—

> " ' Conscienza m' assicura
> La buona compagna chi l'uom francheggia
> Sotto l'usbergo dell' esser puro.' "

" I dinna understand Gaelic," said the president; " I mind my father, puir mon—" ·

But he did not proceed far : there was something so noble in the air and attitude with which this short address was delivered, that an instinctive feeling of surprise and admiration seemed to circulate round the assembly as if touched by some instantaneous electricity of mind. In fact, a rising murmur of applause was only repressed by the president's knocking on the table with the mace. But this was but a momentary pause.

The dark wheel of destiny was not to be so easily arrested in its onward course.

" My lords," cries the secretary, " these documents, you see, contain matter which must be examined into with closed doors : it is my jewty to suggist that the prisoners be withdrawn ; but ere this be done, let me ax whither this nagro baste is the Sazer mintioned in the peepers now before me ?"

Smithers exchanged a glance with the African, and immediately said, " This is Cæsar Clarkson, an emancipated citizen of Berbice, my servant, and my friend."

" Do you admit this, Sazer, my jolly old snow-ball ?" says the secretary of state.

" Ay, ay, Massa," cries the poor but honourable man, and a movement of satisfaction pervaded the board. " To close all," says our hero, " this lad is my guide ; I have him from Holmes's, to shew me the way through London, and I don't as yet know his name."

" Peter Che't'nham, at your worship's service," says the Cicerone; " you may go for to
ax my character at Mr. Robins, he's our head
waiter, please your lordships' honours. I only
come out to let the gemman see the way to ould
Macfarlane's, him as stays in the hellewated
hapartments o' No. 7, Stone Buildings. No,
no, cry your pardon, that there's the young
gemman who's striving to be a bit of a lawyer:
I means him as has that there queer ould brick
house, with them two corcomdiles upon the pilas-
ters; your honours must know the place, 'tis right
opposite the Noll's Head, in Kensington. I'm
a decent lad, please your worships, and can have
the best o' characters from my three last places."

" I presume," remarked a member hitherto
silent, " that we have now heard enough."

" Let the prisoners," (cries another,) " be
kept in separate chambers while the council consider these papers."

" And ironed," says Warrender.

" Yes," said the secretary, " *boulted*, for fear they *boult*," and he laughed at his own pun.

" Od ye're a droll chiel," quoth the chief, " but I see nae need for that."

" Nor I—nor I—nor I," cry several lords, speaking together.

" My motion is overruled," sighs Warrender. " The responsibility rests not with me, damme."

" Parry, my lad," exclaims the secretary, " you have heard his excellency's commands, barring you're deaf."

" I have, Sir," replies the officer ; " and by the splendour of Frobisher, I shall obey them."

" Come, prisoners, right about face—forwards—march !"

CHAPTER V.

On through that gate mis-named, through which before
Went Sidney, Raleigh, Hampden, Russell, More.
                                        ROGERS.*

SMITHERS, after being led through an apparently interminable maze of labyrinthine passages,
was left alone in a small apartment into which a
single doubly-grated window, high up in the wall,
scarcely admitted rays of light sufficient to mark
the character of the furniture. By degrees,

* Though this amiable and good-humoured man is now
chiefly remembered by " Sam Rogers's Jest Book," a work
which appears to have been merely a *jeu d'esprit* of his
youth, yet those who are acquainted with our neglected
literature, acknowledge him a beautiful and indeed elegant
versifier.

however, the eyes of the captive became in some
measure accustomed to the surrounding gloom ;
and he perceived that, by placing a chair upon a
table, he could reach the window. He accordingly did so ; and grasping the iron bars with
his hand, obtained a glimpse of what was passing in a narrow and damp looking court-yard,
oval in shape, and surrounded with buildings of
a singularly dismal appearance. In the door-
way of one of these he observed a cook wench
scouring a fish-kettle, and singing dolorously,
" Di piacer mi balza il cor," with a pathetic expression that thrilled through the sensitive bosom
of the incarcerated Smithers.

Ere long, however, he was interrupted in his
contemplations of the gloomy scene by a pungent
sensation in the *gluteus maximus* ; and looking
round, perceived that a squint-eyed guardsman
was pricking him with his bayonet, as a signal
to descend. To have argued with such a being,

E

would have been not merely useless, but degrading, and our hero complied.

" By jing," said the soldier, " I thinks as how
you must be deaf, for I am sure I hollored to
you ten minutes before I lifted my piece; but
I hopes I have not hurted you bad."

Smithers, disdaining to reply, asked simply,
" What's my fate ?"

" All's ready," answers the Briton ; " I hears
as how you beez to have foin lodgings for
nothing."

" Where ?" cried Smithers, sternly.

" That there's no consarn of mine, Master,"
was the unfeeling rejoinder of the scarlet slave.
" Walk on, Sir," he added ; and Smithers following him without hesitation, they soon reached
a low portal carved in the solid rock, when the
soldier opening a postern with a key of massive
structure, and snatching a lamp from the wall,
informed our hero that he must prepare for a
descent.

They picked their way accordingly down a long flight of steps, and treading a subterraneous arched passage of about a quarter of a mile in length, reached a vault of apparently gigantic dimensions, in which the air seemed to be considerably more elastic. Here Smithers was instantly lifted by two or three rough hands, manacles were clasped around his wrists, and almost before he knew that he was off the ground, a dashing of oars met his ears, timbers groaned and bounded beneath the stroke, an enormous pair of folding doors expanded, and the wherry shot with the rapidity of thought into the open current of THE THAMES. The sudden transition into a meridian blaze of light dazzled his eyes for a moment; after which he perceived that he was placed between two armed sentinels, that Cæsar, similarly bound and guarded, was confined at the opposite extremity of the boat, and that an officer in a magnificent naval uni-

form, seated immediately behind himself, had
the command of the detachments.

Smithers continued to survey in silence the
variegated scenery which this mighty stream
presented, until they had reached a bridge which
spans it about the centre of the metropolis. It
was here that the gentleman behind him, tapping him on the shoulder, said, with an easy
and even playful air, " I understand you have
never been in town before—this is Waterloo
Bridge."

" So called," he replied, " after the great
victory of Wellington, I presume."

" Even so," rejoins the officer ; " do you not
think it a magnificent structure ?"

" I do," says Smithers. " Pray what are
the names of the other bridges, of which I begin
to descry the outlines ?"

" Blackfriars and London," was the answer.

" Ha !" says Smithers, " methinks there

ought to be a Trafalgar bridge too, since there are so many."

" You are not the first that has made that remark," says the other, thrusting his fingers deep into the contents of his quid-box.

" But now the prince is all for the land service,
Forgetting Rodney, Nelson, Hood, and Jervis."

" Is England," continues our hero, " so un-just—for ungenerous would be too weak a word —is England so unjust as to prefer the transi-tory comet of her military, to the unsetting sun of her naval greatness?"

The sailor made no reply, but handed his box to the prisoner, who, of course, accepted the courtesy as it became him. This commenced a conversation, which increased in interest with every inch that the boat advanced; but as it was chiefly conducted in the French language, for, the purpose of veiling the sentiments and opinions it expressed, we shall not attempt to give it in detail. Suffice it to say, that our hero received from his new acquaintance many hints both as to the past, the present, and the future, which in the after course of events proved of eminent benefit to him. It was not, he now perceived, from the Carribean colonies alone that the proud supremacy of the English tyranny was menaced. A wider line of circumvallation had been drawn around the citadel of lawless power, and the question was not whether millions should arm themselves in the conflict, but what nervous hand should commence it.

The anticipations to which these suggestions could scarcely fail to give birth, were, however, chilled not a little when the wherry glided under the first dark shadows of the

" —— towers of Julius, London's lasting shame."

A deep sepulchral gloom rested here on the sublambent tide, whose troubled aspect seemed to present an eternal memento of the tears and

the blood that had so often dyed its bosom.
" From the first Cæsar to the fourth George,
how many sceptre-wielding despots (said Smithers
to himself,) have made these horrid vaults the
receptacles of fettered virtue! What patriots
have languished amidst these damp and vapour-
ous recesses! Pure souls of heroic Hampden,
and martyred Russell! Noble shade of departed Despard! Stern spectres of Thistlewood
and Ings! If yet ye deign to hover over the
scenes sanctified by your unmerited sufferings,
breathe gently as I approach the hallowed spot!
Sustain me, ye immortal influences; be to me
even as ye were to the great heart of Burdett
when the voice of gore rose from reeking Manchester, and *one* Englishman kindled at the
echo !"

It was in such a mood that Smithers felt himself borne rapidly along towards " that gate
misnamed," of which the memory will survive
in the page of romantic Rogers, while poetry is

the language of the heart. The warders, on receiving through the grate the *lettre de cachet*,
which the commander of the wherry presented
to them, caused the gates to be flung back upon
their dank hinges, and the boat penetrated at a
single sweep within the first vault of the fortress.
Our hero being commanded to step on shore,
was formally resigned to the care of the lieutenant of the Tower; and the crew who had
conveyed him took their departure with looks of
sympathy which could not be misunderstood.
Their officer, in particular, exchanged a most
tender adieu and a 'bacco-box with Smithers.
The gates re-opened, the boat bounded once
more into the current of Thames, and the face
of society no doubt soon obliterated every trace
of painful feeling on the one side. Alas! it
was very different on the other.

The lieutenant of the Tower, a man of on the
whole a most ruthless aspect, informed his prisoner
that he must be contented with such accommo-

dations as might be afforded ; hinting in a word
that nearly all the apartments assigned to state
prisoners were at that crisis occupied. " By the
holy," said he, " they're as thick here as rooks
in the ould rookery of Kilmacthomas. Your
name, my lad o' wax, I persave is Smithereens."

" Smithers," replied our hero, emphatically,
and with an air of native dignity that would
have repelled any one save an Hibernian—but
the Major heeded it not.

" Smithers,—a nate name euough to open a
pew door with. I think I remember a name-
sake of your's in Trinity, when that old buck of
a father of mine, the Bishop, was commander-in-
chief there. By the twist o' yer tongue you're
likely to be a yankee doodle."

" I am a MAN, Sir," was the answer. " I
was born beneath the canopy of the western sky,
in the land discovered by the ill-treated Colum-
bus ! But the starspangled banner claims me
not as a subject, though I hail as a patriot the

glorious domain over which it floats in streaky
triumph.   I was born at Cuckold's-row, within
half an hour's walk of Point Shoulder of Mutton in Jamaiky, and I hope I shall never disgrace that romantic land, the very name of
which kindles glowing emotions in my soul."

" Cuckold's-row !" said the Major.   " No
doubt the place is well named, as your father, I
suppose, honest man, had his own rasons for
knowing.   But you need not get into a huff, my
friend Smithereens—Smithers, I mane—at my
taking you for a yankee—for I know very dacent
fellows yankees, who had as little of an Ould
Bailey look about them as if their fathers had
never got the wink from the Recorder.   But
I'm wasting time.   So, I'll just report you, and
you'll know the result in a crack."

Smithers bowed in submission ; and the officer
strode magnificently away, his long ironsheathed
sword clattering sonorously along the hollow
passages of the corridor.   Our hero and Cæsar

were left standing in an open court-yard under
the care of a small party of military.

Ere long a swarthy corporal approached from
the interior of the Castle, and bade the prisoners
follow him. They did so, and were led through
several wards, each more gloomy than the other,
until, at length, they reached the great quadrangle, an area of vast expanse, in which a scene of
comparative loveliness and animation met their
view. The superb menagerie of the kings of
England had, from malignant political motives,
for ages been kept in this the chief strong hold
of their authority; and the huge and massive
dens of the wild beasts, formed of blocks of granite of the most gigantic size, and barred with
enormous bolts of brass and iron, had attracted
a crowd of gazing spectators, that nearly filled
the nether end of the square. The bellowings
of the furious tenants of those awful caverns re-
echoed like thunder among the lofty walls and
towers around them; while keepers shouting,

children screaming, and females in hysterical
agitation, doubled the confusion. Our prisoners,
however, were not suffered to linger here. They
were marched onwards, and halted only when
they had reached the opposite extremity of the
quadrangle, where also a considerable assemblage
of onlookers had collected, but around a spectacle of a very different description. A troop
of dismounted dragoons were practising the ex-
ercise of the broad-sword beneath the inspection
of a square-built, bandy-legged officer, whose
very slovenly dress presented a strange and re-
markable contrast to the stern precision of his
air and demeanour. There was a patch, neither
short nor narrow, on the left knee of his grey
pantaloons; his boots had obviously been *foxed;**
and a very shabby surtout or cassock of blue
cloth exhibited no epaulettes whatever to denote
the regimental rank of the wearer. A button

* *Foxed Boots.* See Vie privée des Anglais, tom. IV,
p. 551.

having given way, the back flap of an unem-
broidered cocked hat or *chapeau-bras** dangled
loose upon the collar, and the folds of a huge
neckcloth, which had once probably been white,
appeared arranged in a manner that would have
caused the bosom of a Nichol† to thrill with indignation. But the compact and rigid massive-
ness of the countenance—the bronzed cheeks,
aquiline nose, and eyes of more than aquiline
brilliancy—the picturesque simplicity of the short
curling hair and whiskers, both of which were
as white as wool—and the extraordinary quick-
ness with which, while the left hand rested on
the pummel of a beltless sabre, the right played
a basket-handled rattan about the knuckles,
elbows, and skins of the more awkward soldiery
—these were circumstances which could not but
arrest the close observation of so shrewd a spectator as Smithers.

* *Chapeau-bras.* Ibid, tom. 1, pp. 50, 371, 403.
† *Nichol* of Jermyn St., the first neckclothier of the
period. See Vie privée, tom. 1, p. 70.

To this person, after a brief pause, the lieutenant of the Tower advanced, and, touching his
cap with the forefinger of his right hand,* said
some words in a tone not audible where our
hero and his faithful negro were stationed. The
officer addressed turned round on the instant
and clapping a small pocket glass to his right
eye, while he shut the left, surveyed the prisoners with a singularly earnest glance of scru-
tiny. This, however, was but for a moment;
he dropt the glass and said something to the
lieutenant ; but his tone also was that of a whis-
perer, and the result of the deliberation or the
command, whichever it might be, was all that
came to the knowledge of Smithers. He and
Cæsar were marched into a wide saloon, the
walls of which were bare stone, and the only
window an enormous skylight. A simple bench
of uncovered fir-plank was all the furniture of

* See Antiquités Militaires, tom. 3 ; also the Trim Papers,
vol. 2. p. 55. 4to. edit.

the dreary hall; and here the lieutenant and his party having wished our exiles a good morning, the huge oaken door, thickly studded with copper-headed iron nails, was closed on those unfortunates, with a clang that thrice reverberated throughout the wide vault above their heads.

Smithers cast his eyes upwards at the last growl of the echo, and became sensible that a sudden change had overspread the face of nature. Hitherto, as has been intimated in the course of our narrative, the weather had been particularly fine, the blue serenity of a cloudless sky had lain in repose and brightness above the towers of London, and Thames had reflected the untroubled gorgeousness of a glowing sunshine from his placid bosom. But now a contrast not to be overlooked presented itself. As if called together by the momentary waving of some magician's rod, an army of clouds, large, broad, thick, lurid, inky, and tremendous, had gathered themselves over the fair face of the

heavens.   Noontide was dark; the gaiety of
the spheres appeared to be wrapt in gloom; the
skylight over the heads of our hero and his
African having lost several panes, heavy drops
of dark iron-gray-coloured rain began to descend
upon the subjacent floor, which being composed
of broad, smooth, white-washed flag-stones of
the hardest quartz, every single globule left a
deeply marked stain, not only where it smote,
but, around that spot as from a centre, diffused
first a sparkling, and then in a wider circle a
spray-like influence. A solitary sparrow, who
had been flitting gaily about the beams, now
composed herself on one particular corner, and
folded her wings in a pensive fashion. The
wind meantime moaned above. Smithers, and
whistled beneath his feet from many a hitherto
undetected cranny.

Ask not the fate of Cheltenham! His knowledge of London rendered him an object of dread,
and he died pierced by five mortal wounds in the

gloomy subterraneous dungeons of the admiralty. None dared to inquire into his fate, and when his mangled corse, enveloped in a sack, was taken up at Deptford, whither it had been wafted by the tide, the spectators of the bloody sight merely shook their heads in terrified silence.

CHAPTER VI.

And if I do not may my hands rot off,
And never brandish more revengeful steel
Over the glittering helmet of my foe !
                          SHAKSPEARE.

Fierce wars and faithful loves shall moralize my song.
                          SPENSER.

WE gather that our prisoners remained to
gether in this wide and waste saloon for the
space of two hours, during all which time the
storm continued to rage with undiminished
violence.   The floor, in short, was quite flooded
underneath the ill-glazed aperture already
alluded to, ere a sentinel entered, and desired
Smithers, and Smithers alone, to follow him.

Our hero, squeezing his good African's hand, obeyed ; and having passed along a narrow corridor of considerable extent, arrived in a guard-room crowded with soldiery, some of whom were playing at drafts, others smoking tobacco, and a few uniting both of these laudable occupations. The sentinel who conducted Smithers led him past these various groups, and tapping at a small door covered with green baize, and adorned with brass-head nails, said, " Here we are." With this he laid his hand upon Smithers' arm, and opening the door shoved him into an airy, cheerful-looking apartment, furnished in a style of the greatest simplicity, a plain wooden table, and two cane-bottomed chairs, were all the moveables he could discover. The table was, however, a large one, and upon it, there lay open, or partly so, several maps of extensive dimensions, with pins stuck here and there in them ; to say nothing of a pewter pot with porter

frothing above its rim, and a plate of the com-
monest stone ware, or English porcelain, containing a slice of brown bread, a small lump of
double Gloucester cheese, and half a dozen raw
onions ; an ink-stand of horn and brass, with one
of Brahma's* patent pens dipped in its lateral
orifice ; various portfolios of black and red
leather, and a despatch box covered with green
morocco, at the centre of which a semi-circular
out-bulging excrescence exhibited a key-hole of
quaint and arabesque design, and over that an
imperial crown in gilding, with the letters,
C. T. L. in bold relievo.—Behind this table
there extended zig-zag-wise a screen of six folds,
about eight feet high, and garnished all over with
paintings of the English masters, Haydon, Gour-

* *Brahma's pens.* The Kentucky transactions (vol. 4.)
contain a curious inquiry as to which of the novels of the
Brambletye series were written with these pens. By the
name they are evidently of an Indian origin.

lay, Cruikshank and others. Here you might
see the immortal Napoleon the First, set forth
(O noble hostility) under the guise of a baker,
with a shovelful of gingerbread kings and grand
dukes, just drawn out of the oven, while Sheridan
in pimpled pride stood by upon a shelf, as yet
unbaked. There the martyred Caroline of
Brunswick, painted in such colours as oppression would fain daub over all its victims,
appeared in the act of examining some special
statues, to which a hideous caricature of the
much misrepresented and heroically devoted
Bergami was pointing her attention with a
ring-girt finger. On one side the pencil of some
unprincipled limner, (let us hope that the tra-
dition which ascribes the enormity to a Lawrence
speaks falsely) had dared to place before the
eye of more than infantine credulity the philan-
thropic Joseph Hume, dissecting with his own
hand the pale and bloody corse of a brither of
his own illustrious house; while opposite to that

a cartoon scarcely less revolting to every feeling of propriety, exhibited the philotheric Martin, the Wilberforce of the quadruped operatives, in the act of shooting several christian friends on account of some transactions connected with a contested election in the county of Galway.

The sentinel had retired, and finding the apartment quite untenanted, our hero had by degrees stept round the table, the better to scrutinize these extraordinary performances. He had been doing so for some minutes with much intentness—for there are moments in which the merest trifles can withdraw the mind of man from the most appalling weight of misery, and such moments came as frequently perhaps to Smithers, as to any other fine spirit that ever dignified earth with sorrows patiently borne—when a faint, long-drawn sigh reached his ear, and he began to suspect, that after all there was some individual quite close to him on the other side of the canvas. The sound recurred ; a third time the sigh was breathed forth with yet deeper intonation. No, there could be no mistake about the matter, unquestionably there *was* somebody behind the screen.

Nor in truth did the unknown long remain concealed. Smithers standing with his head half-turned round towards the left shoulder, saw first a nose, and shortly after the remainder of the figure gradually develope itself, and step forwards towards the table. He recognized the officer who had been drilling the dragoons in the court of Lions; and gently edging himself round within the indentation of the screen in which he had for some minutes been standing, so as to face the table, but still without leaving the zig-zag, awaited in silence the moment in which his fate was to be decided.

The officer in the plain blue surtout, however, appeared to have totally forgotten the circumstances of the case. In fact, it seemed as if he had not the slightest suspicion that Smithers was in the room.

He ate some fragments of the bread and cheese before him, crunched an onion or two, and finally lifting the porter pot in his left hand, took a long, deep, and earnest draught of its contents. Replacing the lightened pewter on the board, he then retreated some yards, gazing all the while with a most melancholy fixity of eye, on a small statue, fabricated by an Italian artist, which our hero had not hitherto observed, but which in point of fact, stood conspicuous enough upon a high and projecting mantel-piece within a few feet of the table. It was upon this tiny piece of sculpture that the officer continued for some moments to rivet his resplendent eyes, until whether from physical straining or internal emotion, tears slow and solemn burst from them. over his manly cheeks.

The blood rushed into the noble countenance of Smithers, as the thought flashed upon his mind that he had unconsciously been betrayed into the position of a spy. But it was too late ; to retreat was impossible, to remain was only torture.

" Ha!" cried the unknown, dashing the brine from his cheeks with a large and bony hand, which seemed to have grown hard and dark amidst the earthquake breath of an hundred battle fields—" Ha !—is it come to this—to this—to this ? Aye, so it is ; even so ! hum ! ha !"

After a pause, he thus continued—" Thou dwarfish mimicry of manhood, by what accursed charm hast thou left the board of thy peripatetic artist to thus unman me ? Nay, keep not thy arms folded in that calm contempt upon thy plaster bosom ! Openly and boldly did I spur my good horse against thee, but I thought at least that duty blew the trumpet which impelled me to that fatal charge ; but never, O never, did I bare the secret knife, never did I brandish

the jailer's key—frown not, thou pallid shade,
confound me not with a Lowe !"

In saying so, the officer laid his right hand
upon his heart, and cried aloud, " Heaven
hears me, Napoleon, Heaven attests my tale. I
fought against thee, because I believed thee the
eternal enemy of freedom and of man. If I
was wrong, Heaven will even forgive the error,
nor should the manes of a hero dwell upon it in
inexpiable wrath.

" I am innocent, Napoleon, I am innocent—
let these tears be my witnesses"—and the stern
soldier lifted up his voice and wept.

He was still lost in this trance of agony, when
a young and lovely female tript lightly into the
room, and gliding between Smithers and the
duke, without perceiving the presence of the
former, laid her hand gently on the shoulder of
the latter, and whispered softly but quite audibly,
" Fie, fie, my lord : your grace forgets yourself.

Are these paroxysms to be of eternal recurrence ?"

He turned half round, and wiping his red eyelids with the edge of his scarf, and finishing the contents of the pot in an agonizing gulp, said, with a faint attempt at a smile, " Forgive me this once, my darling, I had sad dreams yesternight. But 'tis all over now—yes, yes, Harriette, I am myself again—quite myself. Leave me, leave me, sweet maid ; I will attend thee on the instant in thy bower."

The pale girl turned with a sorrowful wave of her hand from the suffering man, and her eye fell full upon the figure of Smithers. " Ha !" cried she—" treason, my lord duke— treason !'

The unknown wheeled round impetuously, and unsheathing his sabre, said in a fierce tone, " Traitor ! thine hour is come ; be thy prayers brief!"

" Hold, hold, my good lord," interrupted
the damsel—" let not the sword of a hero be
stained with the blood of a caitiff!"

" Thou say'st aright," he replied, dropping
his point; " let him find a fate more worthy of
his baseness. Who art thou?" he continued—
" speak, wretched thing, what is thy name, and
who hath suborned thee to play the eavesdropper within this royal fortress?"

" My name," answered our hero, in a tone as
calm as the other's was vehement, " my name is
John Jeremy Smithers, and no eavesdropper,
nor the suborned instrument of any man's baseness; but an innocent stranger arrested, he knows
not why, by the Lord High Admiral of England, and conducted, he knows not by whom,
into this chamber, where, as he understood, the
cause of his imprisonment was to be revealed to
him by the keeper of this castle."

" Ha !" said the unknown, as if striving to
recollect himself—" Smithers ! Smithers—of a

surety methinks I have heard that name ere now—"

" It is a name," proudly replied the youth—" which has been dignified by all the virtues of humanity. I inherit it from a patriot, a martyr, a hero !"

" Did your father serve in the Peninsula ?" quoth the unknown.

" Never, never——"

" At Waterloo ?"

" My father never drew sword of flesh, nor mustered beneath the banner of carnage—the blood of a slaughtered saint cries aloud for vengeance, and Heaven will hear it !"

" A saint !" quoth the other—" a slaughtered saint ! Rash youth, see that thou sportest not with *me*—knowest thou in whose presence thou standest ?"

" I do not," says Smithers.

" Behold, then, Arthur of Wellington, constable of the Tower."

The first impulse of Smithers was to kneel; but a moment's reflection chased that unworthy thought.—" My lord," cries he, " I respect the genius of a great captain, however I may protest against the cause in which it has expended its energies; and I am proud to know that my fate, whatever it is to be, depends upon no vulgar arbitrament."

" Young man," replied the duke, sheathing his weapon, " there is that about thee which seems to merit better things; but let me read the warrant." And without delay he began to examine the contents of one of the boxes on the table, and after a little, unfolding a parchment scroll, read it through with attention and replace it where he had found it.

" Sir," he resumed, " this case is a serious one; you are charged with coming to England for the purpose of communicating with the Irish insurgents, on the part of the rebellious negroes of Berbice. The warrant says, that papers of

the most suspicious tendency have been found
in your keeping, and you are committed here
until you can be acquitted or condemned in due
course of English law."

" So be it," says Smithers, " I am innocent,
and I am prepared."

" Meantime," continues the constable ; " no
discretion is left with me : you must be confined
in solitude, nor can either pen, ink, or paper be
allowed you ; but as to all others, trust me, Sir,
it will give me much satisfaction to consult your
personal comfort.   There is, however, one consideration which I must impose."

" Name it, my lord," cries the victim.

" Swear upon this blade," says Wellington,
again baring his steel, " swear upon this blade,
that thou wilt never, under any circumstances,
reveal to mortal ear what thou hast heard in
this chamber, while I believed myself to be in
my privacy."

" I swear," cries Smithers, solemnly pressing

his lips upon the sabre—" I swear to respect the sanctity of imagined solitude."

" 'Tis enough," says the duke, laying the sword on the table; " you shall have the best dungeon the castle may afford."   In saying so, Wellington struck the bell, and a sentinel entering upon the summons, said, " Here, Fitzroy, take this gentleman to the White Tower."

" One word, my lord," said the victim of tyranny.

" It is too late," said the duke.

" One word, and no more," reiterated Smithers, in a tone of energy.

" Be brief then—Fitzroy, stand at the door," said Wellington, "speak now what you desire."

" I'm devilish hungry," said the hero, with a voice of deep emotion ; " I have eaten nothing to speak of for the last four hours."

" It shall be looked to," said the duke.   " I shall order the purveyor of the fortress to send you a supply of whatever dainties you please."

'Pork and molasses, then, my lord; but ah! I forget that the Atlantic rolls between me and that happy land where only that dish is to be procured. Some tripe," he said, after a pause, "and a few pounds of bullock's liver."

"I grant it—but REMEMBER!" said the duke. The sentinel returned, Smithers exchanged a glance—(it was but one — yet what volumes did it not speak?)—with the lady—bowed to the constable, and followed the dragoon.

END OF BOOK I.

BOOK II.

CHAPTER I.

Like people viewing at a distance
  Two persons thrown out of a casement,
All we can do for your assistance
Is to afford you our amasement.
We see men thrown from a high story,
  And never think the sight's so odd,
Whether the patient's Whig or Tory
  But take things as it pleases God.

                CAPTAIN BASIL HALL's *Crasy Tales.*

THE traveller who, smitten with the natural
ambition of visiting scenes rendered illustrious
by the recollections of famous men of old, visits
the solitary shores of Tiber, Seine, or Thames,
and filled with proud though melancholy

thoughts, revolves over the glorious deeds of a Scipio, a Napoleon, or a Nugent, may in his wanderings through London have noticed that green lane which leads towards the presidential residence of the Protector of the Trinobantine Republic—the chief state of the great Anglican federation. That lane in the days of which we speak was called Bond-street*, and was the favourite resort of the conviviality which so much distinguished the days of King George the Fourth. A celebrated wine-house, over which swung, in all the splendour of gilding, a gorgeous likeness of the renowned Lord Clarendon, executed by the famous Sir Benjamin Haydon, was the haunt of many a wit of those times. The Boniface of these vaults,

* So called from General Head *Bond*, discoverer of the Pampas, and Hetman of the Gauchos. The Rev. Dr. Toddy is wrong in deriving it from *Bonds*, which signified in these days stocks or bills of change. The place where *that* business was done, was in the Royal Exchange on Tower Hill.

Jeronymo Jacquiero, was himself a pleasant,
cheery, Falstaff-looking fellow, a fit specimen
of the hosts of those times when England deserved the name of merry. Seated upon the
broad stone bench outside his door, you never
missed the goodly man, cheering his rotund corporation with a mug of stout, and a pipe of pig-
tail. Near him was seen the jolly form of Sam
Rogers, ever ready with his joke; and still in-
separable here, Lords Alvanley and Aldjo join-
ing in the jovial song, chased away the dulness
of London fogs, by potations of London porter.
The goodness of this last article in the house
procured it the custom of the bishops, and the
presence of so many reverend persons seated at
Jeronymo's door, really made the stone slab
above mentioned (as Rogers delighted to say)
" an Episcopal bench."

On the day when the events which have occupied the preceding book took place, Jeronymo
was inside his tap, when Sam Hodges came in.

This singular and eccentric man was never
seen by strangers but with astonishment. Nature,
which made him by profession a punster, seemed
to have intended his very person for a sort of
joke. He was about four feet high, and his
head was at least a quarter of that size. It
hung heavily to one side, and his countenance,
of an unearthly paleness, drooped like an overgrown turnip hanging upon a pole. His under-
jaw projected considerably, and gave him the
appearance of a perpetual grin. His lack lustre
eye shot its leaden beams from under shaggy
eye-brows, and his locks, untamed by brush or
comb, hung in grisly knots over his wrinkled
brow. Lord Byron, with that disregard for
decorum of language, which so conspicuously
marked the conversations of that celebrated
poet,* used, rather blasphemously, to call him
a caricature of a crucifixion. Strange being!

---

* See Conversations of Lord Byron, by Captain Pimp,
p. 337, 349, 362, 411, &c.

Yet, under that odd and repulsive appearance,
he possessed wit unbounded, jocularity un-
ceasing, deliberate courage, magnanimous phi-
lantliropy.   Sage in council, jocose at table,
valiant in action, luxurious in ease, he was the
idol of London.   Wherever he went, joy
brightened every countenance, and the very
phrase, "it is a saying of Sam's," became pro-
verbial to express the highest degree of wit.   In
this particular, indeed he was unequalled : none
in fact approached him, except the illustrious
Hallam, who, we are informed by some of the
principal critical works* of the age, wrote a

---

* Morning Advertiser, vol. 48, folio 201. Pierce
Egan's Life in London, vol 13, fol. 97. Westminster
Review, vol. 3, p. 9. Rambler's Magazine, vol. 6, p. 118.
We may remark that Archdeacon Ignares blunderingly
calls this gentleman Balaam, which however is not his
name, but the title generally applied to his books.   He is
the same gentleman mentioned by Lord Byron in Engli h
Bards and Scotch Reviewers, as—

"Classic Hallam, much renowned for Greek ;"

jocular treatise on the middle ages, which has not come down to posterity, but which in his own generation appears to have excited an universal laugh whenever it was mentioned.

"What, ho! dish my wig! my bully-rock, my old lad of the castle," said the host, "is this you?—So, my old mouser, you're here at last."

"As sure as death," said Sam, with a sidelong inclination of his head to the right.

"What will you drink, my cock-of-wax, my Trojan, true as ever whistled. Ale, wine, beer, brandy, rum, rack, grog, punch, flip, purl, lambswool, half and half, mum, brown-stout, perry or cider. Speak, you Anthropophaginian —speak, I say, dish my wig."

"I am for some of your old rum," said Sam. "You know I am of the Ecole Rum-antique."

he having very much distinguished himself by a severe cutting-up of the Greek of Pindar, which obtained him a reat deal of glory.

Jeronymo filled him a bumper, which soon
disappeared from the face of the earth.

"Supernaculum," said Sam. "I dub thee,
Jeronymo, Magister Morum."

"Ay," said the host, "old chanticleer of the
roost, as much more rum as you like. But
what's the news?"

Sam was preparing to answer this, but the
entrance of a soldier of the Grenadier Guards
prevented the necessity. He was a tall man,
standing six feet four inches, with a countenance
indicative of determination, if not of ferocity. A
circular mark, in which the blue colour had begun
to yield to the yellow, round his left eye, testified
that he had not long before been engaged in
personal rencontre; while the pustulary ex
crescences that disfigured his aquiline nose,
shewed that he was not less accustomed to the
combats of Bacchus than those of Mars. He
wore a fur tiara, of enormous dimensions and a
conical figure. A pewter plate, indented with

the royal arms of England—gules sable, on a
lion passant, guarded by an unicorn wavy, on
a fess double of or argent, with a crest sinople
of the third quarter proper, and inscribed with
the names of several victories, won or claimed
by the household troops of England, proved him
to be a member of the Horse Guards. A red
doublet, with a blue cuff, cape, and lappelles, was
buttoned with mother-of-pearl buttons reaching
from his waist to his chin, where they were met
by a black leather stock, garnished and fastened
by a brass clasp, on which was inscribed, *Dieu
et mon Droit*, the well known war-cry of the
English nation. White kerseymere trowsers,
buttoned at the knee, and a pair of D. D. boots
—as they were called, from the circumstance of
their having been invented by a Duke of Darling-
ton—completed his dress. His arms were a
ponderous cut-and-thrust sword, with a handle
imitating a lion's head, sheathed in an iron
scabbard, that clanked as he moved along. Over

his shoulder was slung a carbine, or short gun,
which military law required to be always primed,
loaded, and cocked. A pair of horse-pistols
were stuck in his leathern belt, and in his hand
he bore a large spontoon, or pike. Such was
the dress of the *Hanoverian Horse Guards of
England at that period; and such, even in se-
condary occasions, their formidable armour; for
the absence of the hauberk, (or morion) and of
the ponderous target of bull's-hide and ormolu,

* See Cobbett, vol. 317. p. 1248; ibid, p. 716. (note)
&c. &c. Consult also Sir Francis Burdett's Ode to Earl
Canning, stanza 37.

Nor pass, dear friend, the dark array,
Beneath their mercenary sway
    The blood of England flows,
Base instruments of despot's ire,
That trample in insanguined mire
    Britannia's virgin rose.

Their hands the iron fetters forge,
By whose fell means the tyrant George
    Keeps freemen's spirit dumb;
What time from whiskered Gottingen
(Immortal thanks to Canning's pen!)
    To London town they come—&c. &c.

showed that the gigantic Hussar was not at present upon actual duty.

"Tousand teefel!" vociferated the soldier, "give me ein glass of shnaps. Ich bin as dry as——"

"As Dudley's last speech in the Lords," said Sam, interrupting him.

"Here, sourcrout of Almain," said Jeronymo, "here my old jackboot of Germany, put that into thy gob, with a murrain to thee, thou prime cock of the mall."

Fritz Esterhazy (for this was the German's name) threw a sequin upon the board, and receiving in change two roubles, a toomaun, five piastres, a bob and a tizzy, which he immediately deposited in his left holster, drank off the gin with a firm though tranquil air. Replacing the vase out of which he drank upon the table, he sighed heavily. No wonder that he did so: he had just come from the Tower, where he had been attending the sanguinary duties of the guillotine, which had that morning dropt on

the venerable neck of Jeremy Bentham, by the
fierce orders of the stern Sturges Bourne. ·

" It is evident," said Sam, " that this is a
Grenadier of *sighs*."

" Donner and blitzen," said Esterhazy,
" what, for a schelm, is dis ere ?"

" A Paphlagonian Troubadour," said Jeronymo, " hero of Hanover, if ever such was in
Byzantium of Thessaly, an old batterer in the
wars of Troy. Ay—by the belly of Saint Bene-
dict, a Christian of the true church, if any
ever emptied a pot—a man of action, bully rock,
a lad of the game."

" Hold there, old Greek of the Spiggott,"
said the poet, turning a quid in his jaw—" a
truce to thy quips and thy cranks, with a ronnion
to thee. Sir," he addressed the soldier, " my
name by baptism is Samuel, by contraction
Sam."

" Hark ye," says Jeronymo, lifting himself
on tip-toe to reach the soldier's ear, " did you
never read in the bible of that Samuel, com-

mander in chief of the people of Israel, that the old badger of a witch of Endor, who never shaved but once in three weeks, raised by art of magic and hocus-pocus jugglery out of his wooden surtout, to frighten the Queen of Sheba ?''

A deadly paleness overspread the manly countenance of the bombardier. His knees shook, and his under jaw dropped ; but soon resuming his wonted courage, he laid his hand upon his matchlock, and addressed the punster in these words :

" Ihr Engelen von himmel gnade uns bey- standen ! Bist du ein heiliger gheist oder ein feind von dem abgrund ? Sprechen sie, sagich im Christus name—Sprechen sie du unendlichste gestalt ! What is what brings you from the dead ? Are there no Bow-street officers in Lon- don Stadt, to hinder dead mens from walking about the strassen ?"

" O, powers of pewter," quoth Jeronymo.

" What a gibberish ! I never yet could make
out the reason why those foreigners can't speak
English. I know I spoke it at once without
any teaching—dish my wig, but they must be
damned stupid sons of sea-horses," and he
emptied his capacious pot with a smile of satisfaction.

" Truce," said Sam, " to this nonsense. Here,
bully rock, a half-crown bowl—I am a loyal
subject, and like to keep always under the
crown—some clean pipes and no prate."

" Amen !" responded the Hanoverian, smooth-
ing his grisly beard ; and drawing out an enormous tobacco-box from his capote, he presented
it to the poet. The black-jack was soon spiced,
and the trio sat down to partake of its fragrant
contents at one of the oaken tables that filled
the immense area of the tea-garden. Enveloped
in the smoke of their pipes, the three friends,
for such we must now call them, contemplated

through the leafy foliage of the vernal boughs, the insect tribes of men, moving with noisy step and laughing aspect, along the glittering boulevard below them.

" A song, Sam, my sweet singer of Israel," said Jeronymo, after a pause—" lift thy chin out of thy winding-sheet, and give us a stave."

" I should be sorry to think I was a *butt*," was the answer.

" Sapperment, I am sure thee has ribs enow," said Esterhazy, rubbing his brawny hand down the attenuated form of the poet, who composing his features into their usual good-humoured smile, and helping himself to a bumper, which he drank off with a smack that was heard as far as Crockford's, commenced the celebrated ditty of the saintly Montgomery—

" There was an old woman behind the door,
" Her husband was sitting upon the floor," &c.

of which he had just completed the third stanza

when he was interrupted by the agonized voice
of a female. She was singing—

> " Where is my love that came over the sea,
>   " Smelillu—Smelillu, whack foll de roll,
> " A fine strapping fellow of six foot and three,
>   " Sing the green willow shall be my girlonde."

" What maiden is this?" said Jeronymo,
starting up.

But before he had gone a pace from the table
she had burst into the garden. Her height rose
to the majestic, yet every motion, even deranged
as she was, was redolent of elasticity and grace.
Her complexion was of that clear and radiant tint,
which the pencil of Titian has sometimes *approached.* Her eyes, large and lustrous, gleamed
with a maniac splendour, which however could
not entirely extinguish the intense loveliness of
their natural expression. Her lofty brow, white and
cold as marble, was partly shaded by luxuriant
dishevelled tresses, darker, sleeker, and glossier
than the plumage of the new-born raven. Flow-

ing garments of cyprus and black-satin, negli-
gently thrown on, betrayed more of the symme-
trical loveliness of her form than was perhaps
consistent with the prudish notions of that
highly artificial period. Wild flowers, such as
dahlias, rhododendrons, camella-japonicas, sola-
num-tuberosums, quimolias, dandelions, gowans,
and emperors of morocco, which the unfortunate
damsel had gathered in her progress through
the blooming parterres of Hatton-garden, were
arranged fantastically among her locks. She
rushed forward, and twining her long and delicate fingers among the venerable elf locks of the
songster, chaunted, in a high and clear tone—

> " Bloody old fellow, come from the dead,
> Lillibullero, Bullen a la :
> Where has my lovely Creole fled ?
> Lero, lero, Lillibullero, lero, lero, Bullen a la !"

" Something has turned her head," said Jeronimo.

" I wish she would take her hand off of

H

mine," replied the indefatigable bard—" but"—
starting up, as he got a clearer view of her
features, he exclaimed in a melancholy tone,
" Can it be? Is it that peerless girl—is it Lucy
Hawkins—the fair, the angelic Lucy—Oh yes,"
he added, with a deep-drawn sigh, " it is indeed
luce clarius."

" I thought, just now," said Jeronimo, " you
said her name was Hawkins. Poor girl!"

Her sad strain recommenced—

" O, if I were a little bird to build upon his breast,
" Or if I were a nightingale to sing my love to rest,
" To gaze upon his lovely eyes all my reward should be,
" For I love my love, because I know my love loves me."

Tears burst from the iron eyes of Esterhazy,
who, exclaiming, " O mein Gott, was fur ein
hübsche mädchen," ladled out the last relics of
the bowl, and presenting the goblet to the fair
unfortunate, said, " Trink, trink, mein herz, das
make the bauch warmer, trinken sie immer
fort im Gottes name."

" Sie sind sehr höflich, mein herr," replied Lucy, in the purest Saxon accent, and accepted the offered beverage, which she had no sooner drained than her whole countenance, neck and bosom were visibly suffused with a purpureate glow; and springing with the grace of a Gazelle several yards to the right, she snapped her fingers towards the astonished Hodges, and sung:

> " Fy, let us a' to the wedding,
> " For there'll be lilting there,
> " For Jock'll be married to Maggie,
> " The lass with the gowden hair."

Suddenly reverting to the melancholy expression, she screamed rather than sung :—

> " O saw you my father,
> " Or saw you my mother,
> " Or saw ye my true love John ?"

" Not I, by gum, Ma'am," ejaculated Jeronimo. " I don't think as how I ever seed the young man since we turned him off last Lammastide—that is, you mean John, the hosler, fair pearl of Pomerania."

"John the ostler, base caitiff, slave! Unhand me, miscreant. I speak of Smithers—O—O—Smithers—Smithers—Smithers—Smith——"

And she fainted.

CHAPTER II.

The first, the very first, oh ! none
Can feel again as *they* have done
In love, in war, in pride,—in all
The planets !

LL. D.

WE return to our hero.

It was night. The exhausted spirits of the captive were at last folded in the mantle of Nature's repose. The straw pallet, the slimy floor, the lizard-stained dank walls and roof, the narrow oriel high up amidst the entablatures of the dungeon, through which alone either sun or star could send one gleam of light to the eye of Smithers—the heavy chain, the grinding manacle, the filthy pewter pan, with its filthier

water—the refuse of the Dolphin*—the greasy
little plate of Worcester-delft ware, with the crust
which indignation had disdained to masticate—
(for though the duke had, with perfect good
faith, ordered the delicate viands of bullock's
liver and tripe, as he had promised, they had
been intercepted by the ferocious Irish major,
who had devoured them with unrelenting jaws,
regardless of the wants of the captive)—prison-
house and its accompaniments, all were alike
forgotten.

His dreams were deep, but fantastic. Now
the airy power transported him to the mystery
of some far transatlantic wilderness, where, a
young hunter, bounding from rock to rock
beneath the gloom of antediluvian mahogany,
he tracked to his lair the infuriated tiger; or, a
bold angler of the primeval stream, he hooked

---

* *Dolphin,* i. e. The poisonous water of the Dolphin
River, then used in London—the same which was supposed
to produce the terrible pestilence of 1830.

some giant crocodile of the wave, and rode the writhing monster to the bay which his gore was to saturate with the crimson draught of death. The visions of maturer years succeeded, or mingled themselves with these infantile forms. Lonely and wild was the thyme bush beside the gushing fountain of the snow-crested Cordillera, where the voluptuous breath of noon played on his cheek : while close to him, upon the perfumed herbage, lay and panted the angel breast of Lucy Hawkins.

"Heaven of Heavens," he muttered audibly, "do I hold thee in my arms? Is this truth, or am I deceived? O sweet maiden! confess that this is no delusion—confess, confess, angel, darling, my love,—love—love—"

He started suddenly from the embrace of slumber, and raising himself on his noisome couch, perceived a fair, mild face, mournfully bent over him. The lady held a lamp in her left hand, while the fingers of the right held together on her bosom

the up gathered foldings of a resplendent
drapery.

A tear stood in either eye—her lip was pale,
and trembling—Smithers gazed in utter stupor
on the heavenly vision.

" Azrael !" he said at last, " I know thee !
Strike, angel of repose ! O, Azrael, never did thy
icy dart transfix a more yielding bosom ! Spirit
of the tomb, I am ready."

" So you really take me for Azrael, the angel
of death ?" said the fair one, smiling on the
prostrate youth—" upon my word, Mr. Smithers,
I thought you would not have forgotten me
quite so soon, *mon ami*—but who were you
dreaming of ?—Come, tell me frankly—*dites
moi, mon cher*."

" Never," answered our hero.

" Prepare for the icy dart, then," said his
visitant—and she dropped part of her mantle,
and tapped his forehead lightly with an ivory
fan, which its folds had previously concealed.

"I am ready," said Smithers, gaily.—"To be serious, Madam, will you have the goodness to state the purpose of this very unexpected condescension?"

"In one word, Smithers," replied the lovely creature, "from the moment I saw you in the Lord Constable's chamber I felt a deep interest in your fate. It is in my power to break these fetters—arise, and be a freeman."

"What!" cries Smithers—"what do I hear?—*I* escape, *I* creep like a caitiff out of the bonds of tyranny—*I* leave it to be said, now and hereafter, that I stooped to avoid the penalties of wrong, by profiting by the compassion of a woman! You do not know me, fair stranger!"

"'Tis well"—she answered—"I knew it would be so—I made the offer but in sportiveness—But come, I have a real proposal, and I hope to that you will readily assent."

"Speak," was the laconic reply.

"Hear'st thou not," she proceeded, "this rush of chariots, this trampling of steeds, this

tempest of brawling objurgations among coach-
men and cads, and the crowded menials of pomp?
—See'st thou not, even here, the red reflection
of a thousand flambeaux? Does not the distant
violin send one note to thy pillow?"

"Lady, my senses, like my principles, are
still mine own."

"Then rise and follow me. This night, the
Lord Constable has summoned all that is noble,
and wealthy, and gay, and potent in the land to
the wassail. I have brought a mask and a domino
—arise, and array thee. It shall be mine to thread
for thee the mysterious corridors of the fortress—
it shall be mine to place thee in the centre of the
magnificent scene—to point out to thee the rulers
of England, on whom thy fate must in the issue
depend. It may be of considerable advantage
to your case, that you possess a clear knowledge of
the features and motives of your future judges."

Smithers made no answer, but to extend his
ponderously chained arm from the straw of his
lair.

" Here," said the lady, " I have provided
for all that. Take this tiny key. Apply it to
the mid link of each fetter, and they will all confess its mastery. This small portmanteau, which
I placed at your feet ere you awoke, contains
every thing necessary for your disguise—arise,
and obey."

A blush mantled over the hitherto pale countenance of the youth. The lady perceived and
appreciated his feeling; and silently turned her
back towards him until he had completed his
toilette. This being at last accomplished, she
took up the lamp, opened the door of the cell,
and glided away before him into the yawning
blackness of the vaulted gallery of the donjon
keep. Smithers, wrapped in his novel weeds,
stepped lightly after the maid.

She seemed well acquainted with every winding angle of the devious way. " You must be
cautious here," said she, just before they entered
a vault, from the roof of which a lamp swung
dangling, fastened to an iron ring—" for that

spiral opening at the top, which seems intended
merely to carry off the smoke of the argand,
really leads up to the very ear of mon general,
and he is watchful, *comme quatre.* But I
suppose he is too busy dandifying himself just
now. However, caution is the word. Take off
your shoes as I do."

So saying, she stooped down to unloose her
sandals, in the course of which operation she
displayed a beautifully turned pair of ancles.
Looking archly in his face, while the light
from above, streaming down her animated countenance, gave her a most bewitching appearance,
she seemed to call his attention to her pretty
legs. But it was in vain. The image of Lucy,
as before, was present to the eyes of Smithers,
and he saw not what she did. Taking off his
mocassins, he followed her through the treacherous vault.

" I appreciate this favour," he thought, for his
mind was too delicate to utter it ; " but if she
expect my love, she is deceived. I wonder who

she is; or by what means she has obtained such power over the stern mind of the Lord High Constable."

"We may talk now," said she; "this portal leads to my chamber. Stoop, for the passage is not of the highest. But what are you so glum about? A penny for your thoughts, as the Marchioness says."

He smiled, and replied,

" I was thinking then of you."

" You flatter, you coaxing rogue. Well, you Mulattoes are irresistible. But what were you thinking about me, if the question is fair?"

" The object of it, beautiful maid," said Smithers, bowing with a native grace, that went to the heart of the incognita, " is fair. I was wishing that I knew who you were."

" O, pish !" said she, colouring slightly, for she expected a different answer. "I thought every one knew me. I am LA BELLE HARRIETTE.

CHAPTER III.

Silver lamps, like moonlight, fell
    O'er mirrors and the tapestried swell
Of gold and purple :—on they went
    Through rooms each more magnificent.
                              LADY MORGAN.

THEY soon entered her bed-chamber, where
every thing was disposed with all the elegance of
an Anastasius Hope, or a France and Banting.
From a hundred perfumed vases, streamed odours
brought from distant India, groaning at that time
under the iron yoke of a Malcolm,* and his faithless associate, the tyrannical Chundoo Loll. Silks

* The celebrated author of the Sketches of Persia, Baron
Munchausen, and other entertaining romances. My Lord
Canning afterwards gave him the high title of Bahader
Jaw, of which he was justly proud, being conscious he had
well earned it.

of China, shone upon tables of teak, cut in the
subjugated provinces of Arracan. A gorgeous
mirror, framed in silver, dug from the mine of
San Pedro Nolasco, in the snowy Andes, by the
toil of the unfortunate Apire, enlarged, doubled,
and blended the glowing tints of purple and of
gold which shone on every side. A magnificent
chiffonniere or bookcase, of solid marble, the
product of Paros, just emancipated by the illustrious Stanhope, contained, in splendid bindings,
executed by the hands of Absolute John Murray,
the great literary productions of the age. Here
the eye of the student was charmed by the
tragedies of Lord John Russell and Mr. T.
C. Grattan, " teachers best of moral wisdom ;"
the comedies of a Moncrieff stood in delightful
company with those of a Parry, or a Davidge :
whilst, the Epic poems of a Penny, well worth
his name, were next the moral muse of a
Gompertz. The novels of a Lathom, the
historiettes of a Sullivan, the critical labours of

a Praed, decorated the room, and threw over it an air of gay hilarity, which, in the unaffected language of the time, was truly refreshing. Here were to be seen the Memoirs of Lady Caroline, written by herself—here Lord Nugent's political treatises—here the general had placed the military essays of Sir Robert Wilson. In fact, almost all the great and master minds of England had deposited their works in this beautiful boudoir.

" Don't stand gazing, my dear Smithers," said the lady, " I hear the music of the masquerade. Put on this domino*—you had better not assume any character, lest your voice should betray you. And wear this mask"—putting over his head a grotesque representation of the face of a satyr, with a very conspicuous pair of horns.

* *Domino.* A white habit, studded with black spots, so called from its resemblance to the counters used in the game of the same title.

" Is not this," said Smithers, " rather a strange mask ?"

" No, *pas du tout, mon ami*. I can assure you that several of our nobility wear one of the kind. But *depechez vous, depechez.*"

While this was saying, she had put on a sylph-like dress of *leno muslin, sprigged with blue stars representing a Zodiac, and covering her face with a mask of Diana, she again led the way. He followed, and they passed in silence through a darkened corridor, she informing him in a whisper, that she feared to bring him by the usual way. They groped along in the dark for three or four minutes, until an unexpected turn brought them immediately into the great saloon of Apsley House, which in those days formed the eastern quadrangle of the Tower.

The transit from perfect darkness to light almost rivalling day was electric, and Smithers

* See Ainsworth's Latin Dictionary for this word. Also, Vie Privée, Vol. iv. p. 716.

ı

started back. A whisper from his guide, " Be
firm, your life and mine depend upon your
caution," brought him back to his senses ;
and he soon gazed steadily on the wondrous
scene.

It *was* wondrous. All that was great and
gay of London was there. Brilliant dukes,
shining with stars, and glittering with garters,
—valiant warriors and rich bankers honoured by
innumerable orders,—haughty and high-born
beauties,—resistless wits,—luxurious dandies, —
weighty dowagers,—heralds and knights,—sewers
and seneschals filled the hall. Wines of the
most delicious description, sent from the Cape
of Good Hope, or purchased from the celebrated Wright—gin from the great vineyard of
Hodges, or the celebrated Thompson and Fea-
ron, and porter brewed by the immortal Whit-
bread, flowed in abundance. On every one of
the hundred ivory tables spread with luxurious
cates, lights of every curious variety, from tal-

low to gas, diffused a tender perfume over the
room which they illuminated by their splendour.
Every thing was magnificent, in short; yet it
was easy to see by the agitated air of many of
the party, that they despaired of the common-
wealth. The clarion sound, wafted ever and
anon from the left bank of the Thames, fell
sadly upon the ear, for it reminded them of the
near vicinity of the Irish army which had just
conquered Rotherhithe under the illustrious
Sheelanagig, after an obstinate resistance of its
devoted governor, Sir Ruffian Donkey. But the
Duke on this occasion, as on a former one, determined to hide anxiety by the display of mirth.

London was, indeed, in a strange situation at
that period. It was in a manner besieged, and
half of its population was discontented. The
grievances of the subject were enormous. The
massacre of Manchester had not been inquired
into, in spite of the numerous denunciations of
the virtuous Hunt. Arrest on mesne process

was allowed, and the manner of collecting money
by briefs in churches was truly awful. The land-
lords were so unreasonable as to expect rent for
their lands, and the fundholders secured their
quarterly dividends with a ruthless avidity.
Fourteen extra clerks were employed in the
Home Office, though the disinterested Hume—.
the friend of Greece—pointed out the waste of
£79. 14s. 2d. arising from that circumstance.
In the House of Commons the cry of the people
was not heard—even Wood was contemptuously
coughed down. As for the peers, they had
adopted the fatal measure known by the name
of Sixty-six Shillings a Quarter, and dismissed
from their bar the ingenious Wakefield to the
fortress of Newgate. And yet with all these
corroding abominations, the face of things was
gay. Every body admitted that the nation was
ruined; and yet if you visited their palace-like
theatres, to see the tragedies of Shakspeare or
Farley, to weep with Liston, or laugh at Wal-

lack, they were full. The Opera was crowded
—private parties were given in all quarters.
Tattersall's was crammed—Crockford's crowded.
In fact, every place where money was to be spent,
displayed crowds of people, who all could testify
to the melancholy fact that there was no money
in the country. But we wander from our tale.

Smithers became interested in the passing conversation. We shall just give a few scraps of
it, to shew how they conversed in the highest
society in England. If any one should be incre-
dulous as to the correctness of the transcript—if
any doubt should exist, that colloquy so refined
was practicable even in the highest circles—let
them read the delicious novels of Almacks and
High Life, where the contemporary manners are
depicted with so singular a fidelity. They will
be found such as I have attempted to paint
them.

" Nay, nay, nay indeed, my very good lord,

the thing that is impossible can't be, and never, never, never comes to pass."

" *Pardie*, you're a provoking little slut—that you are."

" *Bona verba, bona verba precor;* upon my word, you gentlemen of the Foreign Office give yourselves pretty airs."

" You *shall* dance, you devil."

" Oh, you coaxing humbug, you will always have your own way—La, Fitztruckle! are you not ashamed of yourself? don't pinch my arm *quite* blue—Gad-a-mercy, boy!"

" By jingo, you black-eyed filly, if you don't step out better, the quadrillo will be filled up! Dang me, 'tis even as I anticipated. That doodle, the Marquiss of Hungryville, has just strutted into the only open place with his eternal brokeress. Confusion confound the pair of filthy sinners!"

" Choke the beasts! well, I really *am* disap-

pointed. Let's go in to the country-dance
saloon—come along, there's an active fellow: I'm
determined to have my hop—I'faith the calf of
my leg is all of a quiveration already."

The parties were both masked; but Harriette
whispered to Smithers, who had scarcely as yet
recovered from the surprise excited by the first
coup-d'œil of the gorgeous assembly—" There
they go !—that's an old story ! Well, I thought
Lord Francis would have been sick of the
dowdy ere the second season commenced."

" Honorable depravity !" mentally ejaculated
our hero. " Alas ! alas ! does lawless love thus
dare to bravado it, even in the midst of the con-
gregation ?"

" Listen to this here couple that's a coming,"
whispered his fair guide; " I'll warrant you
they're looking out for some quiet corner. Ay,
ay, that will do."

The two new masks had seated themselves on
the divan immediately behind my hero; some

part of their colloquy could not but be over-
heard, even by the most unwilling bye-stander.
The form and attitude of the female mask, were
magnificent; her hand was ungloved; the slim,
snowy fingers, were laden with a blaze of dia-
monds, beryls, agates, and horn blends. Every
thing in her air and bearing spake lofty birth
and wealth unlimited. Yet she leaned, with a
sort of languid and dejected grace, on the arm
of one whose gestures and voice breathed a
sullen austerity, but little compatible with the
atmosphere around him, and the lady (apparently) of his love.

"Rouse thee! rouse thee!" said the fair,
giving him a smart poke with her forefinger just
in the centre vertebra of the back bone. "What
in Heaven's name, is it that ails thee?"

"Oh! Oh! Oh!" was the responded sigh,
" 'tis all up—the game's done—we're now out,
depend upon it. I know we'll never be able to
manage now!"

" Pooh ! pooh ! my dear lord—what nonsense you *will* talk ! And after all, am not *I* a Whig ? Must you Tories always be *in ?* Fie, fie, you darling !"

" *You* a Whig ! you be hanged !"—was the fierce rejoinder.

" Civil !" resumed the beauty—" Well, is there really no hope of his recovery ?"

" By Jupiter ! his chance is not worth a hair of his ugly old beard—dang it, what business have people in that situation to play such tricks ?"

" Come, *mio caro,*" whispered the lady, " you forget yourself—*uno pulsat pede*—you remember the rest of it—the poor man could not help his misfortune.   Will —— be prime ?" she added.

" I don't believe it.   He ought to try—but he's deucedly in earnest about *the* humbug :— that's the truth on't, my love; the man's a spoon. There's nobody else cares a fig for it"——

" Don't you ?"—

" Not this," he answered, squirting a quid of pig-tail on the spangled floor of the saloon— "but I'll tell you what I do care about, and that is"——

Here, unfortunately, a haut-boy struck up in the gallery, immediately above the speaker, and the rest of his speech was lost to our hero— after a pause, he caught the following fragment.

" One, two, three, four—that's flat—five, yes, I'm sure on't—six—yes six—seven—upon my perdition I think we shall be seven."

" Yes," replied the lady—" you remember Sir William Wordsworth's fine poem——

> ' But still the May would have her way,
> Indeed, Sir, we are seven."

" Flesh and blood !" growled her attendant— clasping his brows with his hands.

" Hush — hush !"— said Harriette, darting from the side of the bewildered Smithers. In a moment she had seized a harp from one of the gentlemen of the choir, rushed back with it to the place where the passionate colloquy was held, and seating herself in an attitude of the most enchanting elegance, trilled a few notes of prelude that effectually arrested the attention of every ear in the saloon, but two. Those two also, her art was ere long to command. It was thus that the lay flowed.—Smithers stood over against her as she sang, the big tear-drops coursing down his cheeks, until the silk of his mask was through all its texture softened and moistened with the gracious shower.

SONG.

Who will come dwell with flowers and me?
My silver mine is the almond tree!
I have watched the lily unclose,
I have kissed the cheek of the rose!
But I know not which is the sweetest yet—
The white and the azure violet:
I know the breath of the violet well!
I drink the dew of the blue hare-bell!
I wear a wreath of the Cistus flower!

When she had come to this part of her song,
a loud and piercing scream broke it off.   The
cause was soon explained.   Smithers, captivated
by the beauty of the verse, the harmony of the
music, and the charms of the singer, had forgotten where he was, and incautiously removed
the mask, which had become wet and oppressive,
and gazed in wonder on the syren.   Just at that
moment, a tall and burly figure in the disguise
of Cocker, entered the room, and his eye was
caught by the countenance of Smithers.   In a
moment, he exclaimed, " Oh—horror !"

The guests crowded round the new comer,
whose agitation increased to the utmost pitch of
emotion.

" What !" said he, dashing his mask on the
ground, and thereby revealing to the gaze of
the company, the purple physiognomy of Lord
Goderich—" What !" said he, " do the graves
give up their dead—do the tenants of the tomb

walk into our saloons, to remind us of our deeds of darkness?"

" Your Lordship raves," said Doctor Aber-nethy, who was there in the character of Punch; " permit me to feel your pulse : if you will read my book, you will find at page seventy.two—"

" Avaunt, caitiff!" said his Lordship; "gulfed be your book in the bowels of Pyriphlegethon. Speak, shade or demon, what brings you here?"

Smithers, alarmed as he was at his situation, and perfectly unable to account for this burst of emotion, on the part of a man quite a stranger to him, did not lose either his pre-sence of mind, or nobility of expression.

" I am not bound to reveal to you, Sir, the secrets of my mission. I came for justice, and I find oppression; for liberty, and my free-born limbs are girt with the manacles of a slave."

His Lordship appeared to revive somewhat, but said, in a tone of intense agony,

"Are you not then the ghost of Smithers, the missionary hanged in the West Indies, by order of the British Government?"

"It avails me not to deny what I am, and falsehood never stained my lips ; of that great and martyred man, I am the son, not the ghost. My injured mother, who mourns her departed love, prepared his culinary fare by day, and shared his couch by night. Africa claimed her birth, and the name by which she was known is Jock."

An anxious and breathless crowd had by this time gathered round the two principal actors of this unprecedented scene. Lord Goderich soon resumed that fierce courage, for which he was renowned.

"So then," said he, "you ruffian of a Mulatto, it is not to haunt me, but to cut my throat you are come. How did you get into this fortress and this saloon?"

"As for his getting into the fortress," said

the constable, who just came up at the moment, "I can answer, that he is a prisoner on a grievous charge from the Admiralty.   How he got into this room, I must discover.   Fellow," said he, addressing Smithers, "how came you here?"

"Did the question affect myself only," said our hero, "the reply should be prompt as the lightning flash, but it may affect others, and I am silent."

"We shall make you speak," said the constable, in wrath.   "Fitzroy, order the rack in : we shall twist this scoundrel a trifle."

"Bless me," said the Duchess of Arbuthnot to a lady next her, " is Arthur going to bring the rack into the ball room, and torture the fellow before us ?   Well, it is quite new, and must be rather amusing."

"Infinitely so," said the Countess, and she drank a glass of blue ruin.

But he was not destined to suffer.   La Belle

Harriette had been hitherto silent, and appeared to be a spectator as indifferent as the rest of the company; but the idea of her love—for her passion for Smithers had by this time swelled into idolatry—being exposed to the tortures of the hideous rack, overcame her, and she burst forward, overturning Lord Tankerville in her way—

"Spare him, my Lord!" said she, "spare him! I can tell you the truth."

"You, you little fool," said the constable, "what *can* you know of such things?

"But I do," said she. "If I prove to you that I do, will you spare the rack?"

"Ye—ye—yes," said the Duke, "I will; we have had enough of that trinket of late, and there is no use of running a good thing too hard. Well, then, what do you know?"

"Nay, nay," said Smithers, "beautiful creature, do not betray———"

"Hold your tongue, you sooty vagabond, said Lord Goderich, "let the woman peach."

" Why, then," said she, raising her vestal form—" it was *I!*"

Astonishment pervaded the assembly—but she continued—

" I opened his cell with this key (holding it up), and led him through my boudoir into this room. Tyrants, do your worst !"

Exhausted nature here put in her claim. Harriette had hitherto been supported by enthusiasm, but the effort having been made, she burst into tears. The Duke eyed both with furious indignation, for jealousy had entered his soul. He stamped on the ground, and bit his lips with rage till they bled ; at last he exclaimed—

" They shall die—both die—and die this moment ! Let a scaffold be prepared in the court-yard."

" One embrace," said Harriette, " my Smithers, and I die in peace !" and she sprang into his arms.

" Part them," said the Duke, livid with rage

at the sight; and Lord Goderich was proceeding to do so, when a horrible clamour outside
the fortress rivetted the attention of all, and the
Major burst into the room.

" By my word," said he, " but it's fine fun
making cockadoodles of yourselves here, play-
acting for the bare life, when all the vagabones
of London have risen in a ruction agen you,
with a little rawhead-and-bloody-bones of an
ould man at the head of 'em. I can tell you it
was my father's son had the hard work to beat
them off the draw-bridge, and get down the
portcullis, or else they'd have been here, three-
nanalya in the middle of you, knocking you
about as if you cost nothing."

Terror or defiance pervaded the assembly on
hearing this eloquent address.

" An insurrection !" said the Duke; " it must
be looked to. Slave," said he to Smithers,
" you are respited for one hour. Tear that
woman from his embrace, and confine them both

in the topmost donjon of the white tower, loading them both with irons. Away !"

The agents of despotism performed the mandate, and beauty was dragged from the arms of valour. She exchanged a glance with Smithers ere she was pulled out of the room, and, pressing her hand to her lips, flung him an impassioned kiss. Is it to be wondered at, that for an instant he felt for her an emotion warmer than that of gratitude? Stern must be the moralist who could censure him, when he saw a lovely female, dragged to prison, and condemned to death for his sake, testifying, even at that dreadful moment, inalterable love, if he for a moment forgot Lucy Hawkins. But fidelity soon resumed its sway, as he exclaimed, with a sigh, " I wish she had never seen me." He had not time, however, for making many tender speeches, for he was almost instantly hurried away, receiving a kick at parting from the ferocious foot of Lord Goderich on the seat of honour, in order, as his Lordship expressed it, to freshen his way.

" Faith," said the Major, " one would take him to be an Irishman, he's such a devil among the girls. And, by my word, he's a mighty nate notion of breaking out of jail. I suppose he had many opportunities of trying his hand at it. But I can't stay idling here, and they playing hell's delights at the gate. However, I would not be the worse for a drop of drink."

The Major then mixed himself a glass of whiskey and water in equal portions, in the deserted ball-room—for all had left it; and the evacuation of the tumbler being concluded, went to the ramparts, where he found the Duke counselling and executing all that wisdom could dictate, and heroism perform. The occasion demanded the full exertion of both.*

* The song (p. 123) is usually printed the other way. The Rev. E. H. Barkerus, O.T.N., with his usual sagacity, has restored the true reading.

CHAPTER IV.

And we'll march up, and we'll march down;
And we cares not who'll oppose us;
And the Orange crew we will pursue,
With the green flag flying afore us.

RIGHT HON. THOMAS, BY THE GRACE OF
GOD, LORD RECTOR OF GLASGOW.

WHILE these doings were carrying on in the Tower, the heroine of our romance, who, the reader must have noticed, has fainted on the only two occasions on which she has been introduced, lay in the Clarendon alehouse, feebly recovering. The three friends continued to carouse, intermixing the flavour of the Nicotian leaf with the potency of porter. They were in eager discussion as to what was to be done in this emergency, when Townsend, a graceful youth of the most taking manners, who officiated occasionally at Bow-street, over-heard them. He immediately suggested the propriety of sending for the poor girl's father and mother, who, he said, he happened to know " voz in Huppa Zeymo-street, wisiting a house what voz near ould Tyburn gallows, next to snuffy Tom Campbell, the wiggy ould Scotch pensioner."

Such, great genius, was the manner in which thy countrymen spake of thee! Those who now, rapture-stricken, peruse thy Ritter Bann, or gloat over the melodious sounds of thy Real-lura, in the civilized regions of Shoulder-o'-mutton or Passamaquoddy, will hardly believe that Townsend, the witty and the wise, the graceful and the good, described the author of these immortal works, the Lord Rector of the University of Glasgow, and beadle of the Cockney College, as being no more than a snuffy, wiggy old pensioner from Caledonia. Such is the fate of talent! But cheer up, young poet—thou, who art now struggling against universal ridicule, whoever thou mayest be—and comfort thyself with the reflection, that perhaps thy poetry will be popular, like Campbell's, when that of Homer and Shakspeare is forgotten.*

Townsend's suggestion was attended to, and he went on his way rejoicing; while the three friends waited in silence the arrival of Mr. and Mrs. Hawkins. They soon came, but the scene between the mother and daughter is too touching to be disclosed. The father appeared little affected, and after shaking his daughter by the hand, and saying that he had no particular ambition to be grandfather to quarteroons, but that if the girl had a fancy that way, she might marry, or do worse, for aught he cared, he descended to the bar, where, with a firmness of nerve which proved that his mind was not moved by the

* Vide Ricardum de Porsono, de Pleasuribus Hopi, in Cideri-Cellaro. Die Saturni. Hor. 1V. AM. Die. nat. Geo. Tert.

calamities of his lovely and interesting child, he
mixed himself a glass of rum and water, warm,
with sugar. There are some souls incapable of
the finer sensations.

The agonized mother cast an angry glance
upon her heartless husband.

"He is killing me, Lucy," said she, "his
cruelty will be my death. A gloomy despair
has seized upon my mind, and I can scarce over-
come it by a regular succession of drams. But
do you, my dear, cheer up, take a tumbler of
punch, with a bit of butter in it, and cover
yourself up warm. The young man may cast
up somewhere, and you shall marry him if you
like. And why shouldn't you? There, there,
like a good child go to sleep, and never mind
being in love for a while. I hope to be giving
you away some fine morning to the young gentleman, and our good friend, little Doctor Phil-
potts, will marry you. I'll dance at your
wedding, I assure you."

Lucy did not speak, but she cast a look of gratitude at her mother that would have penetrated a heart made of adamant or political economy. Vain, however, are the predictions of the human race. Her mother never was destined to witness Lucy's union with her beloved mulatto; for on that very evening the old lady was smothered in her bed. Her epileptic countenance and frothing mouth indicated something wrong. The stomach pump was applied by Sir Astley Cooper, assisted by Dr. Eady, but in vain. The vital spirit was extinct, and her spirit, soaring to Heaven, escaped the murky tenements of the earth. We seek not to dissipate the thick clouds of mystery which overshadow this melancholy event. The rumours of the public, although suppressed by the despotic authority of the Admiralty, were horrible. We therefore dismiss the subject by mentioning that Mr. Hawkins showed no feeling on the occasion—gave his wife a splendid

funeral—and on that day week was married to
Miss Chester, who immediately retired from
Drury Lane. Their after-life was so unhappy,
that she was obliged to return to the stage;
and the success of their celebrated son—a few
years after his mother's death—is abundantly
notorious. Lucy did not hear of her mother's
decease for some time, for reasons which the
reader will soon learn.

"Dish my wig," said Jeronymo, " who's that
rum 'un I see going up there?—I be hanged if
it a'nt Glengall; the best hand at skittles in
England. He won a bowl of punch from me
last week, and I must endeavour to recuperate a
similar quantity of spirituous fluid from him,
anon. Good bye, gemmen; health attend your
potations."

So saying, Jeronymo emptying the pot, hastened after the earl. He overtook him just at
the entrance to the famous skittle-ground in the
flowery parterres of Burlington Gardens, and

they joined in the joyous game. Matter more serious occupied those whom our jolly host had left behind.

Their conversation took a political turn, and they deplored the tyranny under which the nation groaned. They both agreed that a crisis was at hand ; and the soldier declared, that his heart revolted so much at the atrocities he was daily compelled to witness or to perpetrate, that he did not think he could support the government any longer. Bred under the liberal principles of Prince Metternich, his heart inwardly inclined to liberty, though necessity had lent his hand to despotism. He remembered the time when, under the command of the gallant Bismark (whose work on Cavalry was about that time so ably translated by Major Beamish),* he fought for freedom, and he panted to do so once again.

* See " De Arte Puffandi Indirecte, vel per Head-and-Shoulderos." Auctore Henrico Colburno. In newspaper folio, 3591 vols.

When the conversation had reached this interesting part, it so chanced that the naval officer who had conveyed Smithers to the Tower, and, as we have mentioned, sympathized with his sufferings, came into the Clarendon for a Jerry of punch. Sam and he were slightly acquainted, and they fell into chat in the manner then laid down as the regular formula in England—first the weather, and then the ministry. The manly brow of the sailor darkened when political allusions began to be made; and he said,

" Avast! bout ship there; that is enough to make a man of feeling as sick as a cockney, steaming for the first time to Margate."

" If so," said Sam, " follow his example, and unbosom yourself. You appear to be in a strange pitch for a tar."

" Why," said the officer, " that's my maxum:

" 'As for them who's no pity, why I pities they.'

The —— government is as hard as a knot of

oak, and âs foul as the bottom of one of Sir Humphry Davy's ships after a cruise, ———— me if it a'nt."

" I wish then," said Sam, " that our government, if it be fowl, would take to itself wings; —fly away, and be at rest. But what is the exact grievance which makes you complain?"

" Wait till I splice the main brace first a bit," said the tar, " and then I may make you pipe an eye."

" Mein Gott," said Esterhazy, " was for du no tell?"

The much sought for information came at last. The captain having succeeded in penetrating into the internal recesses of the jerry of punch, commenced his narration. As our readers are already acquainted with what he said, we hold ourselves excused from relating it again at length. With a simple but sublime and touching eloquence, heightened by the judicious use of the technical terms so abundantly

supplied by the naval dialect, he related the
arbitrary seizure of Smithers, the felonious carrying him through the concealed arches, the
heavy irons with which his free-born limbs were
manacled, the firm magnanimity displayed by
the master, the ardent and unflinching devotion
manifested by the man; and hinted at the deed
of blood, as yet however but suspected even by
him, perpetrated upon the unhappy Cheltenham. The horror of his auditors may be
conjectured: the pipe remained full—the pot
empty; none thought of whiffling away the contents of the one, or calling for a replenishment of
the other. Grief, wrath, indignation had seized
upon them, and with glaring eyes they sat,
listening to the tale of oppression and of woe.

When the captain had concluded his history,
he slapped his brawny hand upon the table, and
with a solemn air exclaimed,

"Now that's what I call pretty gammon, a'nt
it? My service to you, messmates." And he
drank.

" Ay," said Sam, " such gammon as has never been heard of since the days of Ham, in old times, or of Bacon, in modern. The thing can't go on. Cobbett is right—the feast of the gridiron must be held—nothing can bar it."

" Nein, nein, by Gott," said the German, emphatically, emitting four ponderous whiffs, as he sent forth each word, to the gale.

" But all this wont do," said the captain. " What's the valuation of our staying here spin-ning long yarns over our grog, while the younker is stowed away safe in the hold of that 'ere Tower. Let's think if we could not board it, or smuggle him away, one way or other, in a jolly boat."

The thought was no sooner uttered than it was immediately caught at, both by Sam and Ester-hazy. A long deliberation ensued in the tea-gardens of the Clarendon, as to the manner in which the design was to be executed, whether, in the words of the poet, by open force or secret

guile.* But the opinion of the German here
prevailed. Raising his voice, he sang the celebrated sword song of Körner—that well known
and spirit-stirring ditty, which concludes by the
glowing words:

> And, at last, toll loll in the cor—ner.
>   Toll loll, toll loll de roll, loll toll loll.
>   Toll loll, toll loll de roll, loll toll loll.
>   Toll loll, toll loll de roll, loll toll loll.
> And———— at last, toll loll in the cor—ner.

The effect of which more than Tyrtæan ballad
was electric. Sam, starting up, caught a
spit, which the cook, in a moment of casual
inebriety, had left under a bench, and waving it
over his head, declared he would baste the
enemies of freedom. The naval officer, seizing a
carver, swore by Goles, he would make that into
a marlinspike, which would spiflicate the land-

---

* See Milton travestied, by the Rev. Doctor Toddy, a
pleasant and droll book. It is quite impossible to avoid
laughing at Toddy's part of it.

lubbers. Esterhazy himself, ejaculating as much donner und blittzen as would serve for three pantomimes, sputtered forth flashes of vengeance. Stimulated at last to madness, at least to a pitch of enthusiastic ardour approaching thereto, they arose, and having first embraced one another, performed the war dance with a degree of agility and grace that would have conferred honour on Rhio-Rhio, Madame Poki, and their chamberlain.

Reason, however, soon resumed its throne, and they sat down coolly to calculate in what manner they should best attack the Tower, how and when they should approach, and what troops they should bring against those awful bastions, the very look of which would suffice to affright the most venturous engineer. Indeed, in the reign of George the Fourth, Bergenop-Zoom, the Tower, and Gibraltar, were considered by scientific men to be the three most formidable fortresses in the world, and their military architecture was habitually quoted as being highly creditable to the countries of which they formed the chief pride, and the most impregnable defences.

The three valiant heroes, however, nothing daunted, devised their well-laid plans. We shall soon see how they were executed; it would be premature, as the "gentlemen of the press" say, to give further particulars at the present stage of the proceedings. Succeeding events will sufficiently develope them.

Thus, even in this world, wicked as it is, worth and suffering merit is not always neglected. Smithers, incarcerated in the lonely donjon keep of the White Tower, was mourned by pure love, was passionately adored by illicit affection, and was the object of care to distant valour. As he paced upon the stony floor of his prison, alone in his glory, his eye happening to look through an iron-grated window, rested upon a lovely lunar rainbow, spanning the Thames. It was to him an object of hope. The bright beams of prosperity were about to shine once more through the gloomy darkness of adverse fate, and the bow, with three listed colours gay, was a token of the miraculous union which was then taking measures to effect his escape. His heart lightened, and he sighed no more.

" Shine on," said he, " bright, though transitory meteor. Faint are thy rays, but still faint as they are, they are rays of hope. And are they not now precursors of the orb of day —beams which but forerun the advent of the solar car? May I not then hope that the time is coming when I may look for justice, when my hour of brightness is to spring as unexpectedly from the gloom of prison and oppression, as this rainbow springs unlooked-for in the darkness of night ?"

He gazed in silence on the bow which was fast fading from his eyes, when he heard his name pronounced. Did he dream? No! The word was again uttered audibly, and by a voice which he thought he recognized. He could not be mistaken. It seemed to come from beneath, but how could any voice penetrate that floor of massive stone?

"Smithers," at last said the voice, "*comme vous etes bête, mon capitaine.* Go to your *fenêtre.*"

He now knew who spoke, and approaching his grated window by means of a bench which was in the room, he said, as loudly as he durst—

"Fair dame, I wait your orders, but I wist not what to do."

"I am in the cell beneath you," she replied, "and can put my little head through an opening in my grating. The fools have not thought of searching my person, and I still retain the master-key; but, *hélas! mon ami,* I cannot turn the cursedly stiff wards of this cursed doghole into which they have crammed me, though I have been working with all my poor strength for nearly an hour."

" And what can I do, fair creature ?" said our hero. " Manacles load my limbs, and the degrading handcuff curbs the motion of my fettered hands."

" Try," she replied, " if you can get even a finger and thumb out of your grating, and I shall pass you the key."

He obeyed, and with some difficulty succeeded. Two or three ineffectual attempts were made to seize the key, in one of which Smithers felt a very unpleasant sensation (it turned out afterwards that it was his little finger which was cut off), but they were finally successful, and Smithers received through his bars the all-important key. Harriette had found in her dungeon one of the spears of the warriors of Agincour, left there by chance; and her inventive mind suggested to her that if she could fasten the key to this, and forward it to Smithers, he

might be able to open the prison locks, though
she could not. She succeeded: the cutting off
of Smither's finger *par hazard* by the spear,
was indeed an awkward accident, but what is a
finger compared to freedom? Lombard-street to
a China orange!

Having received the key, the first use he
made of it was to unlock his fetters—a tedious
and difficult operation. That point gained,
however, the rest was easy. He unlocked his
door—groped down stairs to that of Harriette
—opened it—fell at her feet in thankfulness,
and all but sunk into a swoon. She raised
him and pressed her lips on his with a wildness
of love. He did not resist—how could he? He
should be indeed a stock or a stone if he had
repelled her affectionate caress at such a moment; but Miss Hawkins was in his mind. His
lips were Harriette's, but his heart Lucy's.

" This will not do, however," she remarked;
" I know enough of this unhappy Tower to tell

you that escape is difficult here, more difficult
than in any other part of the fortress ; for there
is but one staircase that leads to the bottom,
and that only wide enough to permit one person
to pass at a time. This staircase, *mon ami*, is
always guarded by the Sepoys who are brought
over from India, as being more faithful and
fierce than troops of any other description.
We never could get through these infernal Asia-
tics, who are *noirs comme Belzebub*. It is,
however, a point gained that we are together.
I shall go up into your apartment, if you
have no objection. Have you any, *mon beau
mulâtre ?*"

Smithers sighed.

" No objection, kindest of women, none.
Honoured am I by the preference you have
bestowed upon me, but"—and he took her ten-
derly by the hand—" let not your feelings
master your reason—I love another."

Harriette's eyes were suffused with tears. She
looked upon Smithers at first with anger, then

with a glance appealing to his noble nature; at last her natural gaiety succeeded in dispelling the graver passions, at least for a moment.

" *He bien*," she said, " *c'est tres malheureux*. But cannot you have two strings to your bow, I mean two belles to your string. Come, coaxing rogue, we had better lock this door after us, and proceed we to your room. There is some devilish work going on, I am sure, by the terrible bustle I hear. What can it be ?"

Smithers professing his ignorance, fastened the door, gave his arm to the lady, led her gallantly to her miserable dungeon, and locking that on the inside, and her in his arms to shelter her from the cold, he sat in mournful silence. Abroad the noise was becoming more and more terrific every moment. The dæmons appeared to have been let loose, and the sounds of hell were floating upon the breezes of night.

END OF BOOK II.

BOOK III.

CHAPTER I.

While Afric's sons exclaim from shore to shore,
Quashee Maboo, the slave trade is no more.

HORACE SMITH.

CÆSAR had been treated with even less ceremony than his master. He had been thrown
into the lock-up-room,* a miserable dungeon,
seven feet by nine, much resembling that in
which a tyrannical parliament had confined the
illustrious Hobhouse, for standing forward with
noble port and manly pride to oppose their
oppression.

* See Dr. Jamieson, who derives this word from Lok-
man, a hangman. He observes that there is a lock-up
house in Dundee. Had he consulted the works of Sir
Richard Birnie, passim, he would have found that there
was another in London.

The Major, who rejoiced in such scenes, took him to this dungeon of horror, dragging him by the collar with unrelenting fist.

" March after me," said he, " my black bosthoon, in double quick. I suppose it's well you're used to this sort of work, you vaga- bone, in your own country. Were you ever whipped ?"

" Massa, be ver good," said Cæsar ; "him no whip me more nor twice a week, and neber on Sunday, neber. Him say him prayers."

" Twice a week ?" said the Major, " five times less than you deserve, my nate article. Is the tickling a dacent one? I hope he lays it into you well, so as to make you squeal ?"

" No, him floggee wid cart-whip; thirty cuts, then blood come trickly, and him pickle it den wid salt to make well. Him kind massa —him saint, not wicked buckra, what swear at missionars."

" There's your lodgings for you," said the

Major, throwing him in; "it is as black as your own ugly mug, my purty extract of Day and Martin. You need not fear having your eyes dazzled with too much sun; so do not dread the spoiling of your complexion. And you shall get airy diet, lest your wind might thicken. So now I leave you to your meditations,

> ' And blessings on your curly poll,
> John Anderson, my Jo.' "

He locked the dungeon, and departed to bear woe to some other heart pining in this melancholy Tower. Alas! that the nation which produced the sentimental Sterne could have endured such horrors. "Disguise thyself," says that celebrated and tender-hearted man— (never, never will we believe that he turned his mother out of doors, beat his wife, and starved his daughters)—"Disguise thyself as thou wilt, still, Slavery, thou art a bitter draught; and though thousands in all ages have been made to drink of thee"——But why continue to quote a passage already embalmed in the classic pages of Enfield's Speaker, and John Murray's Reader.

" Him Irishman," said Cæsar, when left to himself. " Irishman big rogue, but funny fellow. Him drink like fish, only fish drink water; Irishman drink rum, when him catch him."

Such was the unsophisticated reflection which came first into the mind of Cæsar. " What can we speak of, but of what we know ?" Cæsar had been bred and spent all his life in the West Indies, where rum being the popular fluid, it was consumed by the natives of the emerald isle, the state of whose pockets in general inclined them to adopt the maxim of the venerable Bentham, the hero of Fleet-street, " the greatest quantity for the least money;" and he therefore naturally thought that the partiality of the Irish pointed to rum. Had Cæsar seen him at home, he would have perceived that whatever might be his potations in foreign climes, nature, true to the finer feelings and softer sympathies of man, directed the Irishman to the native.

Do not, however, imagine that Cæsar was without consolation in his dark abode. To say nothing of the excellent principles of religion carefully instilled into him by his master, he had contrived to purloin a bottle of Jamaica from the bar at Holmes's, previous to setting out on this ill-starred expedition. How this escaped the beagle nose of the Major is hard to say, but it was so. Cæsar, when he heard the key turned, and knew his oppressor gone, carefully uncorked the bottle, and turning his little finger in the direction of the North Pole, swallowed a glass. He had no need of any smaller measure, long continued and judicious experiments having enabled him to gauge that quantity. A second attempt was equally successful. A third followed. Nor was it until after the fourth, he

paused from his labours. Letting the bottle slide
gently from his relaxing hand, depositing his
head upon his shoulder, slipping his legs from
under him, were the simultaneous acts of an instant. A loud snoring immediately announced
that Cæsar, yielding to the spirits of rum and
resignation, was clasped within the somniferous
arms of Morpheus.

How long he slept, we know not, but his
dreams transported him across the ocean. There,
in imagination, he danced in graceful attitudes,
embracing the savoury nymphs of his promiscuous affection; there he cooked in thought the
one-eyed herring and the dulcet yam; there he prepared the ample Sangaree bowl, or listened to the
equally ample sermon of his master. Suddenly
a change came over the spirit of his dream,*
and the awful obeah man seemed to arise before
him. With terror he listened to his words of

* See Poetical Works of Captain the Right Honourable
Lord Byron, R. N. Vol. 19,

power, or shook at the dreadful ceremonies of
the necromantic sage. . Before his eyes were uplifted, a form evoked from the earth, the very
Mumbo Jumbo himself, but that vanished, and
he thought a withered crone stood in his place.
His hair, uncurling with horror, shot perpendi-
cularly from his head, a cold sweat came over
his body, and his muscles grew rigid. A voice
sounded in his ear, which said—" Get up,
you black varmint, out o' crib;" and a slight
application of a toe to his epigastric region,
convinced him that he was awake. He started
bolt upright, and crammed himself into the
corner, for he saw the very crone whom his
dream had painted.

A woman, bent double with toil rather than
age, but whose height when erect, must have
been majestic, of withered features, coarse dark
hair, sallow complexion, and bright black eyes,
stood opposite him inside the cell, with a candle
of sixteen to the pound in her hand. She wore

a cap that had once been white, decorated by a
ribband which in former years had perhaps been
black. Her gown of spotted cotton, fastened
round her waist by a blue ribband, hung below
her heels. She disdained the assistance of a
boddice, nor were her feet fettered in their easy
motions by the encumbrance of shoe or stocking.
Her history was as striking as her appearance.

She was a grand-daughter of a Scotch lady of
the name of Margaret Merrilies, who was a
retainer in the house of an eminent justice of
peace in that country, named Bertram. This
lady's adventures are well known, so much so,
indeed, that he who did not know all about
them, was voted, in the days of which we write,
an ignorant and tasteless wretch, as indeed he
well deserved to be. But after young Mr.
Bertram had recovered his estates, she did not
retain her name. It was reported that she had
been shot by a Captain Hatteraick, but erro-
neously, as she made her appearance under

various aliases, in different places, long after that. Finally, after having been employed by several gentlemen, and almost worked to death, she fell into the hands of a respectable attorney, of the name of Smith, in whose employment she lost her brains altogether, and became a mere idiot and a bore. Of her family was the woman whose presence now alarmed the soberized Cæsar.

"Don't killa me, Obi," said the poor slave.

"Obi," said she, drawing up her figure. "I am not O B, nor yet O C. (She had been educated on the Lancasterian system.) Don't be afeared, for I am a woman of flesh and blood, or rather skin and bone."

Of this she soon convinced him, for, to poor Cæsar's horror, she seized him by the throat, and with her bony hand dragged him to the ground, he howling with affright.

"Now," said she, "you see I'm not a ghost; stop your roaring, you black dog, or you'll

have the Tower about our ears. Stop, I say, or
I shall thrust my fist down your gullet, and
listen to me."

With difficulty she calmed the fears of Cæsar,
or at least the noisy expression of them, and she
proceeded.

" I know you wish to escape from this dungeon; that I learnt by an art with which you
are unacquainted; and I have come for the
purpose of freeing you: it is in my power. You
must, however, obey me, and swear to act as I
direct you in all things. I know the god that binds
you, so I have brought it in my pocket."

Putting her hand into this immense receptacle,
she pulled out part of the hoop of a rum cask,
and bade him repeat after her, taking this solemn
instrument in his hand,— ·

> I swear to be true,
> Good woman, to you,
> Whatever you bid me to say or to do;
> If not, may a crew
> Of devils in blue—"

" O ! missis, putty missis, no ask poor nigger to say dat," exclaimed Cæsar, while his teeth chattered in agony.   " Massa say, talk of de devil and him 'pear."

" So he shall," said the indignant old woman, " so he shall, and that this moment, unless you swear after me, as I order you. See, I am going to stamp my foot and he will come."

" O ! missis, me swear any ting," cried Cæsar, eagerly, " me die wid fright to see him big horns and him saucer eyes."

The oath was continued :

> " If not, may a crew
> Of devils in blue
> Through the realms of Old Nick hawl me quite through and
> through."

As this binding ceremony was performed, the Tower clock struck—

" Hark !" said she, " one—two—three—four five—six—seven—eight—nine— ten — eleven— twelve. The moment then is come. My son !

my son!" and her eye kindled with enthusiasm.
" Drop that bottle," she continued, on seeing
that Cæsar was about to finish its contents;
" drop it, I say, and catch hold of me; I must
put out the light—and then——"

She opened the door, and Cæsar followed in
darkness. They had not gone many steps when
he found he was in the open air, and could see
the lights of the Lord High Constable's gorgeous
assembly in the Eastern Tower. The guests also
seemed to attract the attention of his guide, who
shook her hand at them, and said that she
would soon see them dancing a different figure.
They crossed a small paved court, and came to
an iron gate of massive thickness.

" What kept you so long?" said a gruff voice
in a whisper, " Grand rounds will be here in a
minute; make haste, you know our bargain."

" I do," said she, pressing her finger on her
skinny lips, while with her other hand she
slipped into the palm of Sturges Bourne (it was

he who was her accomplice) a double sovereign, just coined by the ingenious Tierney.

" Your path," says he, " lies through the armoury—you know the way—haste then—haste —you will meet nobody there, except, perhaps, the ghost of old Bess. There, I heard the step of the grand rounds;" and he opened the gate. They passed hastily to the entrance of the armoury, which the keeper, bribed by the old woman, had left open, and Cæsar saw with astonishment the splendid and authentic collection of armour which at that time graced the Tower. His guide stopped, and taking a tinder-box from her pocket, struck a light. She appeared to know every recess of the apartment, for she brought Cæsar to a nook, from which she desired him to take a sword, a spear, and some pieces of armour.

" These are wanting for the deed I am doomed to do," she whispered. " This is the sword of John De Courcy, which he wielded in

the fray; this the spear of Charles Brandon;
and here's the armour of John of Gaunt;
conceal these trinkets as well as you can about
your person."

"Him dam heavy, Massa John Cocy's sword,"
grumbled Cæsar.

"Work, then, slave," she cried; "are beasts
of burden like you to growl. Perhaps you will
employ Mr. Martin to-morrow to haul me up
to Bow Street, but I defy you both, caring for
neither of you the valuation of that," as she
snapped her fingers, which sounded like casta-
nets in the silence of the saloon.

Nothing remained for Cæsar but to submit,
and they left the armoury, and again were in
the open air. The old woman, muttering to herself,

> "Three steps from the east and seven steps from the north
> Will shew us the passage whereby we go forth,"

paced accordingly three steps from the eastern

wall and seven from the northern. After two or three unsuccessful experiments, she brought these points to coincide, and there her foot lighted upon a grating. With Cæsar's assistance she lifted up this, and desired him to jump down into the chasm below.

Cæsar hesitated, and no wonder, for he saw no sign of the bottom of the gulph. " No, no, missis, me break my neck ; leap yourself, missis."

" And if you did break your neck, you villain," she exclaimed, " would not that be a more creditable way of doing so than by the gallows to which you are doomed ? I leap after you. If you hesitate, the guards will be on us. Hark, I hear them as it is."

She was right—the measured tread of the soldiers was becoming more and more distinct every moment. Cæsar, impelled through fear of the major, and of the devilish crew to whom he had devoted himself in case of disobeying the

old woman, mustered up courage, and despe-
rately leaped down. To his great satisfaction
he found that the distance was not more than
about ten feet, and he landed in a soft, muddy
substance, in which he sunk up to the hips. In
a moment he was followed by his female companion, who jumped right upon his uplifted
face. One of her feet gave him a black eye, or
rather turned its sable livid. From the other
no accident occurred, save that it knocked out
his four front teeth, two of which, in the
haste of the moment, he swallowed: she apo-
logized, and assured him he should have four
more as good as new put in the next morning
by Chevalier Ruspini. Before she descended
from his face she deliberately closed the grating,
lest, as she said, it might afford a clue to the
manner of their escape. This being done, she
slipped off Cæsar, and stood by his side. After
groping for a while, she found the passage she
wanted; it was arched, but only four feet high.

" Squat down," she said to Cæsar, on entering, " or you'll break your head against the arch," making him feel its key-stone in the intense and rayless darkness. He obeyed her injunction, and in doing so found that it placed his chin just above the oozing fluid in which he was immersed.

" Take care," said she, " you do not squat too low upon your hunkers, for if you do, you'll be infallibly smothered."

" It be dam close here," said Cæsar.

" No wonder," was the reply, " for we are now wading through the main sewer of London. Have courage, we have only about three miles to go through it; but be cautious: neither knock out your brains, which you will do beyond all question if you go an inch too high, nor get yourself stifled, as will as certainly be the case, if you sink too low: keep the just medium, and catch hold of my tail. By active exertions we may be out of this in about an hour."

"Got tam you," muttered Cæsar to himself, but he feared to utter it aloud, and they proceeded cutch-a-cutchooing along their journey, which the old woman enlivened with anecdote and song, suitable to the place. To Cæsar the trip was by no means agreeable, particularly as John De Courcy's sword used every now and then to get between his legs, and endanger his steadiness. Once or twice he dipped into the flood, but the old woman reproving him for his awkwardness, pulled him out again. She knew every nook and cranny of the winding passage. In about an hour and a half, to the great relief of Cæsar, who was heartily tired of the expedition, a light beaming from above, showed that the toilsome way had reached an end. It was, in fact, the sewer grate of the Clarendon, where the old woman had stationed a page to wait with a torch for her. The grate was soon lifted, and they emerged into the yard of the tea-gardens.

It may be easier to conceive than to describe the appearance of Cæsar. Covered from the crown of his head to the sole of his foot with mud, his right eye almost knocked out, his front teeth entirely so, his head bleeding from repeated bruises inflicted by the top of the arch, his shins cut by John De Courcy's sword, and his sides bruised by the armour of the gallant John of Gaunt, it must be confessed that his usual noble air was not immediately to be recognised; and it is no wonder that the page, with the usual petulance of youth, indulged in a smile. His mistress reproved him.

" Stop your sniggering, you Jackanapes," she said, " and take this honest gentleman to be pumped (you will find it refreshing, Cæsar); and put some basilicon upon his cuts. As for his teeth, we can't mind them to-night. Perhaps it would be as well to shave his head—it

certainly would. Do so, then, and put some
raw meat under his eye.—Cæsar, unless you
have a particular fancy for carrying them, you
may here deposit the sword and armour."

"Me fancy, missis, Got tam 'em!" and he
flung the sonorous instruments, offensive and
defensive, on the ground. The halls of the
Clarendon rung in echo, and even the watch-
man was awakened; but in another moment all
was still. The page took Cæsar to the pump,
where half an hour's incessant exertions wiped
off all traces of the sable stains, and he was
then taken into the kitchen to dry before the
ample fire. His head was shaved, and a brown
caxon—unluckily a black one could not be
found—belonging to Jeronymo, put upon the
bald part, for which, however, it was infinitely
too small. His head and shins were plastered,
and his sides covered with brown paper steeped
in vinegar. Seated then upon a stool by the

fire, he warmed his blistered toes; and being
regaled with a jug of swipes, might be considered as tolerably comfortable.

Meanwhile, the old woman, threading the intricate passages, reached the door of the room
where Lucy lay, wrapt in virgin slumber, dreaming of her love. From this the old woman
awakened her; and her sensations may be con-
ceived, when she looked upon the appalling
figure, dabbled in mud, and wielding a sword,
standing by her side. She was going to scream
out, but the old woman arrested her by saying
emphatically, " Smithers !"

" Come you to tell me of my love ?" said
Lucy, gasping for breath.

" I do," replied the old woman.

" Let me then clasp you to my bosom;
dearer to me than if you were dipped in *otto

* So called, from Baron Otto, who invented it,

of roses, which, indeed, is far from being the case," and she embraced her.

"Lucy Hawkins! Lucy Hawkins!" said the crone.

"How do you know my name?" was immediately asked.

"You lay on these withered knees a child, and your destiny has been watched over by me ever since. Do you remember the fortune-teller you called on amid the shady groves, back of Clare Market?"

"I do."

"I am that woman; do you remember my prophecy?"

"Well, too well! and truly has it, at least in part, been accomplished. You said, after a solemn consultation of the cards, that I was to be loved by a black man, who would be in trouble and drink, and that there was a fair woman after him."

" And that last is true. A fair woman is with him this moment."

" Life, then," said Lucy, falling into a flood of tears, " is not worth having;" and snatching a razor with which she used to cut her corns, attempted to sever her throat, but the old woman prevented it.

" Rash girl," said she, " forbear. It is in your own power at once to free him, and to win his love."

" And how—how, Sibyl of my fate ?"

" Do you not, then, remember hearing a voice under your window chaunting a prophetic rhyme ?"

" The voice was your's ?"

" It was."

" O, woman, woman !" said Lucy, in wonder, " how connected you are with my mysterious destinies. The rhyme is fixed in my bosom. Does it not run thus ?—

‘ When a black man is in a tower white,
By a virgin, wielding the sword of a knight,
His enemies will be put to flight,
And valour will link with beauty bright.’ ”

“ You, then, Lucy Hawkins,” said the old woman, “ are the virgin.”

“ But,” asked her friend, “ where is the sword of the knight ?”

“ HERE !” cried her aged companion, in a voice of thunder, as she uplifted the sword of De Courcy in her withered hand. “ Here,” she said, “ take the faulchion of the bravest of knights, the conqueror of Ulster, the champion of England. Here, take it in the name of freedom and of love—take it in the name of vengeance and retribution—take it, and conquer.”

Her figure was drawn up, and her eyes gleamed with a spirit that did not seem her own. Her language too was not that usual in Rosemary-lane, where she resided. Lucy seemed transfixed with awe and wonder; but

soon recovering, accepted the sword that
gleamed magnificently in the light of the bed-
room candle, and began to dress, which was but
the work of a moment. The old woman brought
her then to the kitchen, where Lucy kissed
Cæsar in a transport of joy. She would have
asked a thousand questions about his master,
but the old woman did not allow time to be
wasted. Three skilful armourers, who were sent
for, altered in a few minutes John of Gaunt's
armour so as to fit Lucy; and the sword
being buckled to her side, and the spear placed
within her grasp, the young and the old woman
mounted on two palfreys, which had been led to
the door.

"Cæsar," said his conductress, "you must
go back the way you came."

"Me be tam first," said the sable son of
Afric.

"Remember your oath, you vagabond," said
the old woman, in a mild, yet energetic tone.

" If me took as much oats as two, three, five horses, me not go back dat dirty march. Me no care for your devils."

The quarrel was now growing serious; and Lucy inquiring into the matter, interceded for Cæsar; who was taken into favour again, on condition that he would go, as Lucy's squire, on her dangerous errand. How he was to go was now the only source of embarrassment; but Lucy, with her usual tact* and good feeling, arranged that point by setting him on her saddle, and riding behind him, as was then the fashion of the day for ladies of rank. Thus, with Charles Brandon's spear in one hand, and her other arm clasped round the waist of the interesting name-sake of the hero of Pharsalia, she proceeded to the Tower, the old woman leading the way.

* Tact. See Brougham's Speeches, Vol. I. p. 3, 5, 7, 9, 11, 13, 15, 17, 19, 21, &c. &c. Ditto, Vols. II. III. IV. to XXVII.

Who this old woman was—why she took this interest in the business—whence she obtained her information, and procured her power—may be disclosed hereafter.

CHAPTER II.

Instantly rose a shout, a riff-raff-ruffianly roaring,
Hullabulloo immense, a most voluminous volley.
FROSTY-FACED FOGO, ESQ. BY THE GRACE OF
GOD, POET LAUREATE TO THE FANCY.

Down with the rogues and the robbers,
Down with the vagabonds cruel;
Pepper their phizzes with jobbers, .
Twist your shillelah, my jewel.
THOMAS MOORE, ESQ. BY THE GRACE OF CAPTAIN
ROCK, POET LAUREATE TO THE ROMAN
CATHOLIC ASSOCIATION.

THE preparations made by the soldier, the punster, and the sailor—(why should we any longer conceal the name of the latter, when it was LORD COCHRANE, hot from the liberation of Greece? Glorious man! whether campaigning among the Greeks of the Acropolis, or

the Greeks of the Alley, thy object was consistent and unvaried!)—the preparations, we
say, made by the soldier, the punster, and
the sailor, were speedily completed, and an
ardent and impetuous army was gathered, and
became impatient to march against " the
Towers of Julius." The skill, with which it
was raised, is deserving of attention. They,
after much deliberation, had determined on
summoning to arms all the discontented in
London, who were not already serving under
other chieftains. Parliamentary Reform was no
longer a topic which could avail, because the
tyrannical Admiralty had left no parliament to
reform. Besides, the ancient Radicals had already hoisted their famous banner, " No
Triangular Parliaments," and were bivouacking
in Stamford-street, with the Japanese legions of
the valiant Hunt. Roman Catholic Emancipa-
tion also was in the proper hands, and Sheelin-

agig had, as we already mentioned, with the
assistance of the jolly Jacklawless, led an
army of the Faith, furnished with flails, to the
important conquest of Rotherhithe, whilome
the city of the famous Gulliver, the President
of the Traveller's Club. Dismissing, therefore,
these trite topics of complaint, which had kept
so many newspaper editors alive for so many
years, they looked to other grievances; and the
foreign nations, at that time living in London,
naturally occupied their thoughts.

The Jews had many reasons to complain.
Arbitrary arrests had incarcerated or banished
the most chosen of the people. The hand of
fate pressed hard upon the Solomonidæ; the
patriarchal Ikey himself, had been obliged to
emigrate to North America, without being sent
there, like the original settlers of that country,
at the expense of government. His beauteous
consort, torn from the happy scenes in which

she had so long dwelt in bliss, was removed to the Australasian dominions, there to contemplate Kangaroos. Reuben Josephs, dragged from Monmouth-street, inhabited the gloomy dungeon of Newgate. The corporation of London had refused to sanction the cow-slaughtering propensities of Samuel Samuels, within the walls of the city; and Mr. Woulfe was let loose to pray upon the lambs of Israel. Nor had there been a Hebrew champion for many years within the ring; and the children of Zion remembered, with the brooding bitterness of ancient hate, the overthrow of Mendoza, and with the indignation of modern anger, the prostration of Philip Sampson. In this last case, insult had been added to injury, for Captain Hardman, the poet, was hired for thirteen pence half-penny, to raise that calumnious song of Christian triumph, which begins with—

" Go back to Brummagem, go back to Brummagem,
Youth of that ancient and half-penny town."

The next body which occurred to our me-
ditating trio, was the Ravagees.*· These gallant
men had been banished from Spain and Italy,
for the mere crime of having fought too bravely
for the constitution of their country.   The
degraded Ferdinand was unwilling that men
who had performed such incredible acts of
valour should remain to shame the recreant
herds of courtiers around him. He, therefore,
by secret machinations expelled them, and
they arrived in the hospitable dominions of
Britain. Here they were so over fed, that, like
Jeshurun in the Scriptures, " they got fat, and
kicked." They demanded that they should
be admitted ·into Parliament, *ex officio*, to
infuse into the councils of England, the same

* Put Slangice, for Refugees. See the Reverend Doctors
Toddy and Jon-Bee, *in voce.*

wisdom, that marked the proceedings of the
Cortes. This was refused, and they, in consequence, cherished great indignation against the
ministry. The Duke of Wellington, it was
rumoured, had hired Jeremy Bentham, to
poison the venerable Romero Alpuente; and it
was certain, that when that great patriot in-
serted three letters in the leading journal of
Europe, the conscience-stricken warrior of
Waterloo did not dare to answer them. Our
conspirators knew, therefore, that they would
find willing auxiliaries in the Ravagees.

The quarrels concerning Passamaquoddy had
alienated the Americans, who were, however,
somewhat patient under that great wrong, until
the unwarrantable conduct of Matthews stung
them into rage. Wrathful and infuriate, they
thirsted to avenge the injuries of the much ca-
lumniated Jonathan W. Doubikins. Matthews,
had long before this time, fallen their victim,

but not satisfied with this individual vengeance, they determined on turning their irritated hands against the nation itself.

Lastly, the Germans had for some time complained of the inferior quality of the beer, and the good-for-nothingness of the tobacco. And at this moment, they were smarting particularly under the infliction of the Foreign Quarterly Review, which they considered as personal against themselves : nor did they pardon the proprietors of the Annual Souvenirs, for having poached upon their ancient domain.

Every plot, in short, laid by the triumvirate succeeded to admiration, and in about two hours the army assembled by moonlight, on the Boulevard of Bond-street. Such an army, perhaps, had never before been mustered in the cause of Freedom and of Man !

Aid me now, O Muse ! Thou who didst give thine inspiration to the noble Chateaubriand,

when he sung, how the French host marched
against the Natchez, in the immortal work
which bears that name. I have to sing of an
army just as respectable.

First, then, on the right of the line, a post
which they claimed from the antiquity of their
descent, stood the tribes of Judah and of
Benjamin. From thy flowery purlieus, O,
Whitechapel, from the famed fountain of Ald-
gate, from the fragrant parterres of Rosemary
Lane, from the Holy Temples of Duke-street,
there poured forth an Eastern host, led on by
Hyam Barnett. The central regions of the
Strand, produced from pun-provoking Wych-
street—from the street which derives its title
from the holiness of its well—a body of people
marshalled by Abraham Belasco, a hero who had
dwelt long in camps and courts. Thou, region
known by the name of the devoted son of Charles
the Second, romantic Monmouth-street! sent out
thy valorous tribes. To them no recess of the

Seven Dials was unknown. To them the ways
of Earl-street, were the paths of pleasantness—
those of Tower-street, paths of peace. From
the lane of Saint Martin, from the very extremity, where Pocknell sold his animals crus-
taceous and testaceous, and where his sister was
a prey of the bigamist, to the region bounded
on the North, by the City of Holborn, on the
West, by what the base punsters used to call
the Robert Southey, that is to say, the King's
Mews, on the South, by the Charing-Crossical
domain of the decapitated Charles, and on the
East, by realms unknown, but gradually melting
into the Hundreds of Drury, there came the
determined Hebræists—the real Masorites.

There were among them those whose venturous finger had dipped into the flap of coat,
or insinuated itself into the pocket of waistcoat.
Among them also were those whose sonorous
voice had offered to public vendition the selfsame
waistcoat, or the identical coat which their bro-

ther Levites had assisted to empty.   Men they were despisers of the authority of Knowlys— altogether contemners of their paid friends who sat in the offices which were jocularly called offices of police.   An odour arose from this quarter of the army which was of a nature not at all participating in that of the essence of lavender.

They had chosen for their chief in the ab- scence of Ikey Solomons, the celebrated Bar- nabas son of the brother of Moses, who was generally known by the title of Barney Aaron. With a field-marshal's bâton, which he had bought at the Duke of Gloucester's sale, he swayed the Israelitish army, marching like their forefathers of old against the towers of Ramoth Gilead.   Behind them waved in the breezes of night, the lion banner of modern Judah—a pair of breeches, fresh from decennial wear.   The standard-bearer, proud of his charge, was Israel d'Israeli, a curiosity of literature

from Bloomsbury.   Next to him on his left,
stood, beaming in sallow beauty, his illustrious
friend, known by the title of Uncle Ben.
While on the right he was supported by
the Right Hon. John Charles Herries, C. E.
who had been, a little before, converted to that
faith by the preaching of his friend Roths-
child.   Rabbi Ganab Ben Zonah, was chaplain
to the host, and chaunted the prayers with all
the melody of the synagogue.   But the minstrel
of the army was Braham, who performed upon
the celebrated instrument of king David, the
Jew's harp, making its tongue of steel, utter
forth notes of silver.   The song of defiance
alternately rung from his mouth, and Israel
heard with delight, the melodious voice of
Braham uplifting the glorious and spirit-stirring
canticle of

> Dish de vay how Shoo he lives,
> Mozhy takes and Mozhy gives;
> Go along Mozhes, pull away Mozhes,
> Purty Mozhes, Mozhes my boy.

The sounds of this heart-rousing strain inspirited the souls of the children of Abraham, and brandishing their jemmies, they marched forward, shouting aloud their ancient war-cry, " Clo, clo."

Next to these marched the gallant Ravagees. Their uniform was simple but elegant. Disdaining the covering of a hat, they suffered their uncombed locks to wave gracefully over their faces, undiluted by water. Their uniform was a green coat, at the elbows of which vent-holes had been generally placed, and in so judicious a manner, as to secure all the benefits of a free current of air. Other garment they had none, unless you wish to give that name to their footless stockings devoid of leg. They were armed with a paving stone in one hand, carefully abstracted from the street under the personal inspection of Loudon Mc. Adam—in the other, a clove of garlick. From the lofty tenements which under Athenian name, surmount the edifices of Orange Court—or from the subterranean dwellings which are excavated below the halls of the city of St. Giles, emerging or descending as the case might be, they moved forward in the cause of liberty. At their head was Romero Alpuente, now 158 years old, having been an esquire to Charles V., when he campaigned against the first Francis of France. The banner of these gallant men was a white feather, carried in proud ostentation, by the valiant hand of Quiroga, hero of the great feat of *Sauve qui peut !* Blanco White, in an archi-episcopal mitre, scattered the smoke of rosin, as incense, among the host, singing forth—

> Tantum ergo sacramentum
> Veneramu cernui.
> Et Burdettum atque Bentum
> Bettymartin all myeye.

Next the chaplain stood the minstrel Veluti, who with manly voice, shouted aloud —

Beggi, beggi, bettra trade is,
  Ti, ti, ti, ti, tal, lal, la,
Thana fighti Frenchy Cadiz,
  High go, scampery, sneaky ba!

Napoli, Espana, runi, runi,
  Raci, chaci, tal, tal, la !
In Britani beggi money,
  Gulli, goosy, ha! ha! ha!

Brave heroes! moved by these strains, you moved gallantly to the combat, the beams of the moon, brilliantly illuminating the naked beauties of your uncovered limbs.

Close to the warlike Ravagees, the American nation was ranked in close column, under the command of the brave sable antagonist of Cribb. This nation wore straw hats, black silk-handkerchiefs, sailors' jackets, nankeen garments which once had been pantaloons, but which repeated washings had shrunk to the more convenient size of breeches and tawny mocassins. Their arms were tomahawks, which they wielded with a deadly dexterity.

Ever true to the cause of freedom, they had
deserted the flowery walks of New Orleans, the
verdant haunts of Charleston—had moved from
Alabama and Point Pigsnout—from Biglick
and Cape Cod. Well the individuals knew
the turns of Bowery in New York, and the
purlieus of Second-Street in Philadelphy.
Among them were some of those noble individuals, who at the same time commanded regi-
ments raised for the destruction of the human
body and kept taps for its refreshment. Led
were they to the fight by Bill Richmond,
the hero of a hundred combats, and behind
him the standard of the States was borne by
Albert Gallatin, whose colour-sergeant was
Stuart Newton, the eminent artist. The
standard was not a flag, but, like the
Roman Eagle, was fixed stationary on a
pole ; it was a Newgate Calendar for the
year 1700, in which was recited the gallant
deeds of their progenitors in house and road,

The Reverend Washington Irving raised the psalm; and the national melody—

> Yankee doodle, doodle do,
> Yankee doodle dandy,
> Yankee doodle, doodle do——
> For the girls they all love brandy—

sung snuffingly from five hundred nostrils. A more imposing body never marched into a field, and as they moved forward, they flung the Nicotian fluid in copious showers from their salivary ducts.

Last came the Teutonic tribes: the Honderspondering Sourcroutian legions. Ample were the breeches of these heroic Allemanians, and their honest cheeks were big with beer. Treuttel and Würtz were elected their chieftains, and Ackermann, assisted by Schoberl, bore their banner—a bunch of German sausages waving in the eye of night. Dr. Kruger kindly volunteered to act as chaplain; and Moschelles, performing on the instrument for

which he was so famed, that instrument called
in the German tongue Der Hurdigengurdigen,
in English a hurdy-gurdy—chaunted aloud
with melodious tongue, Weber's justly admired
air—

Ich bin liederlich
Du bist liederlich
Wir sint liderliche leute,

to the enraptured ears of his audience. Armed
with snick-a-snees in one hand, and mugs of
mum in the other, they deployed upon the left
of the line, valorous in soul, and eager to
shed the blood of the oppressors of a ruined
country.

Such, and so various was the army gathered
by the conspirators. By unanimous acclaim
they appointed Sam Rogers, Generalissimo of
the Forces, and crowned him with a punch·
bowl. His heart swelled with merited pride.
It was no wonder ;

" For never since created man
Met such embodied host."

When his eye glanced to the right, he surveyed the army of Israel, and marked the valiant
bearing of those interesting tribes. There he saw
Sir Menassez Massez Lopaz linked arm-in-arm
with Daniel Mendoza. In another quarter
he beheld Hyman Hurwitz, the fabulist, totter-
ing under the Talmud. Here he saw Samuel
Taylor Coleridge, a proselyte of the gate, who
had lately submitted to the last rites and ceremonies of initiation into the law of Moses, blowing
a ram's horn in the manner of the besiegers of
Jericho. As he turned his eyes along the line
to the left, he was proud to behold the operatic
force of Ebers, headed by the Amazonian
Rummins. The valorous Yankees exhilarated
his mind, and it was impossible to gaze upon
the Teutonic chivalry without admiration. With
a proper care for the health and religion of his
troops, he made Doctor Eady, Surgeon-General,
and the Reverend Mr. Smith, of Penzance,
Chaplain in Chief to the Forces, investing him

with a boatswain's whistle, as the clerical badge
of office.

The signal for advance was speedily given,
and they marched *en échelon* along Piccadilly
to the sound of instrumental harmony.   They
deployed from that spacious area, through
Hyde Park Corner into Stratford Le Bow,
where they were joined by Mr. Cobbett, who
was appointed on the spot Drum-major to the
army, and soon his vigorous arms, waving the
thigh bones of Tom Paine, made the welkin re-
echo.   From Stratford Le Bow, their way led
them into the Strand, where many recruits
joined their standard.   Warren, of Japan, was
chief of the warriors—of the minstrels, Power
and his man Tom Moore shone supereminent
as they danced before the host in Erin's yellow
vesture clad, with chaplets of chopped parsley
on their heads, playing upon the harp that once
had hung upon the walls of Tara.   The Editor
of the Morning Chronicle, received the lofty

office of Bulletin manufacturer by the pound
to the army of invasion.

So general was the disaffection of the
Strandians at this time, that there was scarcely
any attempt to oppose the progress of the insurgents. One, however, there was, and if for
nothing, but thy solitary fidelity—yet even .for
that, O Tiffin, thou dost well deserve to be immortalized in this undying work. When the
tide of revolt had reached Temple Bar, Tiffin,
though alone, closed that strong fortress and
bade defiance to the besiegers.

"Who are you, friend of mine?" said Sam,
when he saw him appearing in armour on the top
of the barbican.

"Tiffin," firmly answered the devoted hero.

The army was mute in admiration of the
gallant man, and awaited the answer of their
generalissimo.

"Tiffin !" said he, "we shall then soon make
a luncheon of you, as the Quihis say, if you do

not let us pass quietly. What are you, that you thus take the liberty of barring the bar, which shows you to be a *barbare ?*"

" Know you not then," replied Tiffin, with a dignified air, " know you not my important office in the royal household ? Know you not that I am BUG DESTROYER to His Majesty— that the bloodsuckers of royalty perish beneath my dexterous fingers ?"

" Then," said Sam, "as you are a cracksman, you should not object to our breaking in. Seriously, my friend, you are acting the part not of a kill-bug, but a hum-bug."

" Traitor !" replied Tiffin, hurling at him a volute which he had taken from the top of the monument, " here I stand ; be faithless who may, my duty, my oath, my honour is pledged that the blood of the King is not to be spilled. His sacred person I defend against creeping traitors."

Sam ducked, and the ponderous stone passing

over his head came plump on the os frontis of
Esterhazy, the valiant soldier, and dashed out
his cerebral fluid. In even train it flowed
gently over his nose, and in a moment, the
gallant grenadier was numbered with the dead.
Peace be to his manes!

> How sleep the brave who sink to rest,
> With all their country's praises blest ! *

With an eye of compassion, Sam surveyed
the corpse of his friend, who had died with the
pious expression of " *Den Teufel, Ich bin des
Todes,*" on his lips, and while a tender tear
trickled over his cheeks, he mournfully ejaculated—

" I never expected to have seen him make
such a display of brains."

Rage spread throughout the host at this sad
spectacle, and they rushed with united impulse

---

* Collins's Peerage, p. 461.

on the fortress of Temple Bar. Tiffin was alone. What then could he do? The Yankees, skulking in lane and alley, flung their toma-hawks at him when he appeared on the ban-quette, and the missile shower of the re-doubtable Ravagees was incessant. At last a simultaneous rush at the gate, (in which no other accident happened, save that old D'Israeli, Standard-Bearer of the Tribes of Mount Zion and Rag Fair, was squeezed to death against the door-post,) forced it open. The fate of Tiffin was sealed. The Jews, anxious for his clothes, and grieved at the loss of their Standard-Bearer, ferretted him out. Long did he fight —but numbers at last prevailed, and he fell pierced by a hundred jemmies, exclaiming " No bug—bug—bug——" His body was taken by Albert Gallatin in his brawny hand, and flung over the Temple into the balmy waves of Thames. Such was the fate of Tiffin !

The obstacle of Temple Bar being conquered,

nothing now opposed the entrance of its invaders into the citadel of Soho-square. This
curious work was generally considered to be the
chief-d'œuvre of Vauban. Treason, however, had
been at work, and instead of enemies they there
found friends. Pickersgill, with pallet in hand,
and red nightcap on head, soon joined their
array—Goulding and D'Almaine contributed
their sackbutts and psalteries—Yates, and his
brother Botibol, speeded to the combat. Thou
wert not absent, O Beazley, manufacturer of
farces—thy feet, O Cochrane, delayed not to
convey thee from the corner of Greck-street;
nor did the dwellers in the white bower, which
graced one of the angles of the citadel of
Soho, linger, when they heard the call of
Freedom and Liberty Hall! Thou, O Payne
Knight, wert low in dust, and Charles Kemble
was wandering within the smiling flower knobs
of his garden.

Descending the lengthened steps which led

from Soho-square, the army came plump in front of the brewhouse of Meux and Co.

(" *Tant mieux*," said the Generalissimo.)

Here the army made a halt, and declared that they would not move an inch farther without refreshment. They immediately made an attack upon the large vat, which was fortunately full of the cerevisian liquor, in spite of the remonstrances and resistance of the elder Meux, who was ultimately flung into the vessel, to give it, as Sam said, " what all the beer in London wanted—a body."

Having thus invigorated their persons, the bold battallions next deployed down that tremendous pass, called Break-neck-stairs which led into the parterre of Green-arbour-court. Here a motley crew of various mixed nations, poured down Bartholomew-lane to join them. These new recruits were composed of Greeks of all nations, whether from Athens and Sparta : St. James's and Pall-Mall, the

Alley or the Exchange, Mexicans and Colombians, Jews and Scotchmen, Philhellenes and those tribes distinguished by the sable leg, were here confusedly mixed. Orlando Furioso led the band, and Crockford officiated as chaplain. Their war-cry was, "Sheventy-foive pe—shent;" but though they all agreed in this symbol of union, a discordant clamour rung along the line, for while one set of Greeks, the heroes of the Acropolis, declared that they rested their hopes on Heaven, their brother Grecians, the knights of St. James's, though equally honest and pious, declared that their preference was towards Hell. This body blended with the Jewish nation, whom they much resembled both in valour and discretion.

At last the Tower came in sight, and the awful note of preparation was struck by the grand drum-major with the thigh of Payne. A council of war was held. The Americans declared, (Bill Richmond loudly dissenting)

that they calculated it was pretty considerably
dangerous to fight unless they were snug behind a wall, for their countrymen were never
known to fight in any other way; and accordingly it was resolved on, that they should en-
sconce themselves at the corners of the neigh-
bouring courts and passages, thence to discharge
their unerring tomahawks, they being themselves out of danger. The Ravagees were
ordered to march boldly under the Tower walls,
and to keep up a well-directed fire of paving
stones on those who should appear. " If five
hundred of these fellows," whispered Sam to
his aid-de-camp, Lord Cochrane, " be knocked
to pieces, it will be no loss." The Jews it was
determined were to steal gently to the gates,
and to open them with their jemmies; and the
Germans were to make a dash, to get in over
the principal drawbridge.

Every thing was arranged without being observed; the inhabitants of the Tower being

wholly occupied with the festival of the Lord High Constable.

"Forward," said Sam; "they may have a tower of strength, our's hitherto at least, is the *tour d'artifice.*"

Their usual war-cry, "Sour crout, sour crout," rung from the Germans, who rushed forward and actually gained the drawbidge. Fortunately for the inmates the portcullis was down, or there might have been for ever an end to the empire of Great Britain. But the outcry did not escape the vigilant ear of the Major, who exclaiming, "Thunder and turf, but there's music! I wonder what is to be the fun next," started up, and summoned his attendants to the ramparts. Instantly a shower of stones, or as the major called them, "two years olds," flung by the hands of the Ravagees, and a flight of tomahawks discharged by the ambushed Americans, fell in among them. Thirty were killed on the spot, and seventy-five wounded by these murderous missiles.

"Faith," said the Major, " but that's a purty salute in the cool of the evening. However, let us try paceful ways first; so just give'm a volley, and then we must see what they want."

At his word, a thousand muskets sent their bullets among the host of the Ravagees. Instantly Quiroga fled and communicated in the western regions the premature and mischievous information, that all was lost. A bullet passed through the body of Veluti; he died, exclaiming with his stentorian voice, " *Popolo d' Egitto,* I die like a man," yielded up his soul.

The major hung out a flag of truce, which being acceded to, a parley was beaten, and he went to the gate, the drawbridge of which was occupied by the invaders. When the chieftains approached one another,

" Why, then, my little raw-head and bloody

bones, what in the name of Ould Nick brings
you out of your quiet coffin, at this time of
night?" said the Major. "I wonder you ar'n't
afraid of getting could. Arrah, go back, man,
to your grave, and tuck yourself up snug and
warm in your winding sheet, instead of coming
here to be bothering us. What do you want,
I say?"

" To demolish this castle—to set the prisoners free—if I must be frank, replied the
Generalissimo."

" Mighty civil indeed," said the Major, " my
purty housebreaker. I tell you what, and
charge you nothing for the advice, take a plain
man's word—to the right-about-face, beat the
chamade, and trot to the tune of the rogue's
march. I suppose you know that music well.
You have no chance of getting in here, I assure
you, until you are brought by a bum-bailiff at
the scruff of your neck—than which nothing
looks more likely."

"Major," said Sam, "you argue like a minor. If you proceed to talk thus about your premises, we can have no middle term. Open your gates, therefore, and submit to my irresistible army of well tried men."

"Tried, no doubt," said the Major, "but not well tried, or they would not be here to-night; long ago their necks would have felt the weight of their heels; so no more at present, from your's faithfully. Talk spoils conversation—and there's an end to our palaver."

The parley having thus angrily concluded, the Germans made an endeavour to scale the portcullis, when by a dexterous manœuvre the Major drew it up, hoisting aloft Ackermann, Yates, and Botibol, who were killed upon the spot; and a body of the most fierce of the Tower warriors, accompanied by all the lions of that fortress, rushed upon the German nation. Dreadful was the combat. The men of the Tower were armed with the long lances which they had found in the armoury; and they alternately succeeded in pushing the Germans forward with them; and in turn the Germans, getting inside the guard of the lances, cut their throats with their snick-a-snees. The Ravagees and Americans looked on, fearing to discharge their weapons, lest in the promiscuous *mêlée* on the drawbridge, they might do as much harm to friend as to foe. Deeds of eternal fame were performed on both sides; nine times in a quarter of an hour the bridge was lost and won, and dead bodies choked the moat. The roaring of the lions was tremendous, but in the mixed mass they were not so useful as was anticipated; the only feat of consequence which it was known that they performed, was the biting off the head of Moschelles, and there was nothing in that. At last the Major was victorious, and he chased the invaders from the bridge, and pursued them to their entrenchments. His valour had been conspicuous in the fight, and his voice floated loudly above the tumult in the pursuit. "Kill the ruffians—crap the villains—tear out his tripes—quarter is it you want, honey? I hav'nt time to quarter you, but here goes off your head, if that will oblige you as well—skiver that vaga-bone—sliver off that blackguard's knowledge box—there you go, my hearties—huzza for the ould Tower Hamlets—Tamaroo!"*

When he had got them into their intrench-ments, he retreated, drew up the drawbridge, put down the portcullis, and closed the gate.

"Stay there, my beauties," he shouted from the ramparts, "stay there, my lads o'wax, cool-ing your heels outside o' the door. I am going to tell the master, and if he does not pummell the rascally souls out of your rascally bodies, call me a cuckoo."

Having made this peroration, he proceeded to report to the duke, as the reader has seen already.

* See the song, "Crickey, how he used to swear—Tamaroo."—Mrs. Hemans.

CHAPTER III.

O God ! O God! O God ! what will become of me!
O dear! O dear! O dear ! O my poor wife and children!
O blood and turf! I'm dying g——
CAPTAIN HARDMAN.

THE clamour, as we have hinted, did not fail to reach the ears of Smithers and his fair companion in incarceration. In vain did they strain their anxious eyes through their grating—it did not command a view of the scene of action. A thought, however, suddenly struck the lady.

" I have heard *mon capitaine*," said she, " hint one evening in his cups, that there is a trap door in the topmost donjon of this abominable white Tower, by which a person could

get upon the platform on the outside. I fear
that it will be of no use to us in the way of
escape, as the tower is too high ; but as it commands a complete prospect of the whole country
round, suppose we try if it be possible to get at
the trap. If we succeed, we shall learn what
this *tintamarre du diable* means."

Smithers proferred his assistance in any way
in his power, and accordingly the lady mounted
on his shoulders, his cautious modesty confining her nether garments, so that her taper
ancle should not be disclosed to the unhallowed
gazing of a male eye. Harriette, muttering
somewhat, of which Smithers only heard the
word " *bête*," sounded the ceiling of the tower
with her lance. After making our hero move
about all parts of the room, for half an hour at
a pretty quick trot, she had the satisfaction
of hearing a hollow sound. By probing dex-
terously, and in a manner which proved, alas !
that she had too intimate a knowledge of the

general practices of these horrible haunts, she
succeeded, in about ten minutes more, during
which time she kept Smithers in a posture of
uniform steadiness, in touching the spring;
and in an instant down dropped an iron ring,
which had been painted of the colour of the
ceiling. The whole had been constructed by
George III, who, after having been wounded
by Margaret Nicholson, became very suspicious,
and retired to this almost impregnable tower.
It was a secret confided but to few, that he
spent most of his time upon this platform, from
which he could see from a far distance the persons of those who sought an interview, which
was granted or refused, according to the opinion
which the King formed of them from personal
inspection. She without delay pulled this in-
valuable ring, and the trap-door came down,
overturning her and her supporter by its
weight. She was unhurt, and the injuries

which he received were trifling, being no more
than the breaking of his nose, and the other-
wise general disfiguration of his countenance.
His eyes and teeth were providentially unin-
jured, and the loss of the ear, which he after_
wards suffered, was more justly attributable to
the ignorance of his surgeon, than to any really
important injury received from the slanting
descent of the ponderous trap.

The ether poured down from above; and
from the moon, reigning predominant in heaven,
there gushed a flood of glory almost rivalling
the solar ray. O! luminary of the night!
why do no poets sing thy praises? Why have
we no sonnets beginning with, O Moon!
—no hymns, which by their being printed with
capital letters at their beginnings, are generally
considered to be verse? Why does Lord Byron
content himself with saying, " Hail, Moon," &c. ?
But thus it is with retiring modesty; it is

neglected, while the —————'s —— —— ——— the
rising sun.*

By the aid of Smithers, Harriette mounted,
and speedily got out on the narrow platform on
the summit of the Tower: but Smithers could
not follow her, and besides, a constitutional
malady had always affected him in the Iliac regions, whenever he heard the noise of fight.
Harriette, he thought in his magnanimous
bosom, stands as lonely in the world, as she
does now on the lofty apex of this solitary.
tower. If a casual ball deprive her of life, her
loss is no more felt in society than that of a
drop of water from the expansive bosom of the
billowy sea. But in my case, my life is valuable, and if I fell, it would be not as if a drop
were lost, but as if the vast estuary of the
Amazons was forbidden to roll its mighty tide

* Vide Sanctum Stephanum, passim. Tractat. var. de
Rattibus, Whiggibus, Toribusque. p. 1, 2, 3, 4, 5,—
usque ad 750. Voluminibb. annuar.

into the breast of the Atlantic. I shall therefore stay where I am.

Having thus resolved, he remained in quietness, awaiting the report of the maiden on the castle top. She had, indeed, a wonderful, perhaps an unparalleled combat to behold. She had taken her position precisely at the most interesting period. The Duke, on proceeding to the ramparts, had ordered the cannon to be pointed on the entrenchments of the besiegers; but, to his infinite rage and disappointment, he discovered that the Ordnance Department in the general corruption had omitted supplying balls, which they had preferred selling to Astley's, Sadler's Wells, Vauxhall, and other places of entertainment,* where the sanguinary taste of the nation demanded the representation of real battles.

---

* See Price's Drury, Kemble's Garden, Terry and Yates's Pilot, with many others. Consult also Vie Privée, vol. vii. p. 219.

With equal horror he discovered that the sally of the Major had exhausted all the powder. It is in difficulties that the great mind is most easily discerned. With a promptitude not to be expected from ordinary men, his grace ordered that all arms in the armoury should be brought forth, ordering for himself the armour of John of Gaunt.

"It is no time, now," said he, on learning that it was no where to be found, "when we are in this dreadful crisis, to make inquiries; but by Jupiter Stator, I shall, the moment the combat is over, cause such an investigation, as that the person who has secretly carried out this armour, will wish he had never been born."

Unhappy coincidence of sound! Sturges Bourne, who did not catch the whole of the sentence, thought that this last word was his name. He turned pale, and his teeth chattered with agony. In a moment the Duke had seized him by the collar.

" Speak, caitiff," said he—" speak on—"

" O, your Grace, your Grace," exclaimed the trembling man, " spare my life, and I'll tell all !"

" Brief, then, villain, brief !"

" I gave them to an old woman, who carried off also John de Courcy's sword, and Charles Brandon's spear. O spare me ! spare me !"

At the mention of De Courcy's sword, the Duke turned pale.

" *You*—dare not name yourself now. The woman was bent with age ?"

" She was, your Grace, she was."

" Capless, and shoeless ?"

" Yes, your Grace, yes."

" Her hair was grizzled, a sable silver, as Liston says ?"

" Yes, your Grace, yes."

"Die, then, caitiff !" exclaimed the Duke, and ere the unfortunate victim could say another word, he flung him over the ramparts into the ditch below. The miserable man was heard for some moments rolling down the scarp, and a heavy squelch, attended by a cry of despair, announced that his mortal career was o'er. The verdict of the coroner's inquest was, " Found Drowned."

" This then is the moment. The hour is come," exclaimed the Duke. " Was it this that was meant by the mysterious man to whom I gave a shilling for telling my fortune in Ram-Alley, Cowcross-street. It must be so. What were the words ?

> In the white tower, by Courcy's sword,
> A lovely lady will be gored,
> Who was much beloved by a lord,
> And the dark face shall be restored.
> The sword shall surely pass away;
> In the hands of bent, shoeless, capless, and grey.

I did not understand the last line until now —but how is the sword to get into the Tower ! It is impossible to tell. I'll think no more. Major," he cried, and that functionary advanced.

The Duke lowered his voice to a whisper—

" Major, I can trust you, I hope."

" Is it me ?" said the Major ; " why by the holy——"

" There is no need of swearing. Obey me in this ; leave the ramparts and go to the foot of the white tower ; examine the Sepoys on guard, as to whether any person has had access to the dungeon in which she—you know whom I mean —is confined ; and if not, keep the watch yourself, I can depend upon your vigilance, and if any one appear with John De Courcy's sword, apprehend that person, be it male or female, old or young; remain there 'till I relieve you in person. Go at once—not a moment is to be lost."

The Major obeyed.

" Very fine oysters," said he, as he departed. " So I must go looking after a petticoat and a rusty ould sword, and bating going on outside as chape as dirt. Well! them women, when once they get into a man's head, knock every thing clane out of it—and why shouldn't they, the darlins ?"

On arriving at his station, he found that no one had passed the Sepoys, and began to pace up and down before the Tower, sighing occasionally when he heard the murmur of the distant fight ; in which his soul yearned to be.

The Duke had hastily armed his men with pikes, half-pikes, spontoons, mangonels, mercisde-dieu, malls, maces, bills, and other instruments of ancient war ; the army advanced, animated by the cheering oratory of Mr. Figgins of the common-council. The American tomahawk again fled with deadly effect ; again the paving stones of the gallant Ravagees, fell *en ricochet* on the covert way of the Tower. Again the sonorous voice of Germany uttered defiance, and the attack general was made up the glacis, precisely at the moment that Harriette ascended

the platform.   It was a glorious and spirit-
stirring scene, and well worthy of the picture in
which it is immortalized by the undying pencil
of Day and Martin.

"I see," said Harriette, "I see, my Smithers, an unheard of sight.   The most gallant army ever human eye beheld, is attacking
this accursed fortress.   Who rides in the front
upon a grey Arabian, I know not, but I take
it to be Death on the pale horse, coming to view
the destruction of this devoted Tower.   Ah!
who are those? Treuttel and Würtz, Guten
Morgen, mein herren—glückliche reise'!   I
knew those brave bibliopoles, *quand j'etais à
Paris, avec mon Colonel.* Behind them march
their warlike countrymen.   But who flanks
them? Their raven locks hang over their taper
shoulders, or their unwashed faces—their coats
are green, and nothing but the balmy atmosphere shrouds the remainder of their limbs."

"That force, Madam," said Smithers, who

had, under the care of Dr. Meyrick, made himself master of all the European uniforms, and
whose youthful soul had been, in the Antilles,
wonder-stricken by the courage and wisdom displayed by the patriarchs* of Spain and Italy,—
" that force, Madam, is the far-famed Ravagees :
the terror of tyranny in Naples and Cadiz, and
of the parishes in London, Westminster, and
Southwark. What weapons do those heroic
men wield ?"

" As well as I can see," said the lady, " they
brandish stones ; and lo ! this moment a shower
of lapidary missiles is falling on the rampart."

" More flinty than these missiles," said
Smithers, " must be that heart, which ——"

" Truce to sentiment, my lovely mulatto,"
said Harriette. " What is this that wings
through air ? From unseen hands a shower of

* Vulgar for Patriots. See Pierce Egan, vol. 35, p. iii.
Dick Martin, Orationes, vol. 7, p. 199. Discours de M.
le Vicomte Chateaubriand, tom. 65, p. 379.

tomahawks comes waving on the wind. Thick
as autumnal leaves fall the men on the ban-
quette."

"What warriors, fair lady," asked Smithers,
"stand forward in defence of England's throne ?"

"To the right you may see," she answered,
"the Bishops of Salisbury and Durham, girt in
episcopal armour, cheering on the troops with
a loud huzza. With them are the champions
of England : Cribb, potent, though in gout ;
Spring, valiant, though in business ; and Scrog-
gins, terrific, though in liquor. In the centre,
Mon Duc, and Lord Goderich, with the judicial
authorities of the law : Best, patron of the fray,
and Grahame, vigorous in a row. To the left
are Birnie, brave and polite, the prince of thief-
catchers, linked with the venerable Halls.
There attend the Episcopalian Bishop, and
the benignant Clements. Various other great
men are sprinkled along the wall. Ah! cruel
tomahawk ! thou hast dashed in the forehead of

Petersham, and his vast quantity of brain is
distaining his manly whiskers. An arrow from
the rampart transfixes the bosom of the scientific Eady, my friend and physician. Alas! his
specific avails him not now!" and she wept for
a moment.

But the harsh times of war do not long admit
of the soft resources of the tender feelings.
" He is dead," said she; " thank Heaven, we
still are left Warren and Larnder."

" How is the war carried on?" said Smithers.
" Does Fortune adverse, or prosperous, wait on
the besiegers?"

" Your question is this moment answered,"
replied his friend. " Victoria! Victoria! We
are free. Chief Baron Alexander, after fighting
valorously, is obliged to fly with the rapidity
of a hare: and Romero Alpuente has knocked
out the brains of Baron Grahame. Arthur, look
to thyself—thou art almost alone. Goderich
gives way—Anglesea totters. But what is this?

Thou *art* alone ! Gallant knight—in vain
dost thou strive. The Ravagees have scaled
the ramparts, and even now pour in upon thy
defence. But useless, it appears, are their
pummelings upon thy jointed armour—the
paving-stones fly off, and leave thee unhurt.
Thou art spattered by the dirt of thine enemies
in vain ; it hurts thee not !"

" Is the Duke then by himself?" asked
Smithers.

" Completely. How his faulchion descends
like lightning ! There goes a head, there an
arm — here is lopped off a thigh, here the
grinding steel passes through a yielding trunk.
O, Ravagees, Ravagees, what is this ! You
fly before one man : useless are your paving
stones ! Alas ! whither do you fly ? Luck-
less men, into the angle of the bastion, which
you are never doomed to scale ! Hark ! heard
you not that cry of horror ? The treacherous
earth, hollowed by the art of the miner, has

sunk beneath their tread; they are hurled down the precipice of five hundred feet deep, and not a Ravagee has escaped to tell the tale. Peace be to their ashes. I cannot help admiring the valour of their conqueror, even though it tells against ourselves."

"Is there, then," said Smithers, "no chance for the invading host—are all enveloped in the misfortune of the Ravagees?"

"Hope" —she cried — "bright, brilliant, elastic hope. The Generalissimo on the white horse, has brought up his heroes to the gate —they have burst it, and Cribb and the Bishop of Chester have been trampled in the entrance. With snick-a-snee in hand, they cut, they maim, they hack, they maul. And— a miracle! A host I did not see before, dark-looking, bearded, and clo-crying, have, as it were, emerged from the earth. Who can they be ?"

"Fair dame," said Smithers, " they must

be the descendants of Abraham.   But on which
side are they.   For the King, or- against him?
Have you looked in the ' Times' of the morning,
to see how ran the state of the Money Market?
An eighth per cent. would make all the dif-
ference."

" I have not seen the ' Times,' " said Harriette,
" the paper I read is the ' Post,' in which the only
part I look at is the fashionable arrivals.   But
they are here against the King.   One of them
has fallen : an ancient Rabbi, to all appearance."

She was right in all she said.

The Jews, while the other armies were engaged, had been actively employing their
jemmies in picking the lock of a low sally-port,
and after some time, had succeeded.   They
emerged, jemmy in hand, shouting as we have
already observed, and as Harriette remarked,
their ancient war-cry of, " Clo, clo."   The
part where they entered was slightly guarded,

and they drove in the picquets before them. A parting shot, however, from a catapult, hastily erected by Mr. Galloway, who had just deserted from the Greeks, hit Coleridge in the forehead, and in a few moments he breathed his last. He died as he had lived."

" We are told," slowly snuffled he, " that the swan floating upon the beautiful bosom of the river Cayster, emits its musical note once only, and that once, when seized upon by the icy and inevitable hand of death. It is a magnificent and sublime fiction, if it be a fiction, which I doubt; for the marvellous of nature hath always appeared to me much more probable than what the prosaic men of an unpoetic age have looked upon to be the common and every-day workings of human life—as if they, prosaic as they are, and regarding things merely as they are in detail, without referring to the original impulses, the holy radiances, the metaphysical naturalities, from which all things flow, could tell

whether any thing in detail, even that which they
saw before them existing, existed or not ; much
less were the every-day workings of that incom-
prehensible thing, called life or not—I say, waving
further discussion on this parenthetical point, I
mean parenthetical in form, though thematic in
substance, and taking it for granted, protesting for
ever, nevertheless, against the assumption, that it
is merely a fiction—it is one of those sublime and
magnificent fictions, which in their essence TRUTH,
are by their adornment exalted into something
not greater than truth; for truth is greatest ;
but into something which, by the strangeness of
the garb, i. e. the imaginative clothings in which
it is conveyed, is calculated to take a firmer
hold upon th mind, than if that which it
meant—supposing it a mere allegorical fiction,
an interpretation against which I have already
protested—had been conveyed in its abstract
form, viz. that pure souls, typified by white
swans, never utter such words of hope and glory,

typified by song, as at the moment of death.
Therefore, as I shall explain hereafter—but, for
God's sake, a glass of brandy and water—therefore, when we consider the ramifications of
idea, that idiosyn ——"

He died: Gillman, of Highgate, sorrowed at
his death: and the grief descended the hill as
far as the Castle, the hotel of the ingenious
Carter, as thou enterest the slope of Kentish
Town.

" There appears to be a new manœuvre going
forward," says Harriette ; " the Germans seem
puzzled ; they have got between two walls,
and cannot scale the second. The Generalissimo is ordering a horrid instrument forward, which he is pushing against the wall.
What can it be ?"

" A battering ram," said Smithers.

" O, yes," said she, " I perceive who are
the corps appointed to play the ram. Well

done, Sir Jacob Astley! But where are the
Jews? Has the banner of Judah departed ?"

She well might ask, for it was nowhere to
be seen ; as usual the tribes had gone into dis-
persion. It was impossible to keep them together, for each went in quest of *swag* and
*toggery.** A great opportunity was thus lost.

While they were in quest of antiquarian
breeches, and antediluvian coats—while their
fingers were nimbly examining, whether a half-
penny lurked in the pocket, or a note had
carelessly remained in a fob—the Germans had
established themselves in the space between the
two glacis of the Tower, and were heard at work
battering at the inner rampart. Had the tribe
of Judah been at its post, its lion banner, the
ancient inexpressibles, might have witnessed a

* Hebrew for plunder, and old clothes. See Jon
Bee's Hebrew Lexicon. Also Collectanea Solomonica,
and the Reverend Hartwell Horne.

victory over the host of Wellington. But they loitered too long over the prey, and the moment was lost for ever. Suddenly a cry was raised that the Tower was won, and the Americans advanced, perfectly convinced that there was now no danger; and, according to the usual custom of that chivalrous nation, they went forward slick right away, pretty considerable and tarnation valiant, we calculate, in the manner of him never to be named without honour and glory.* Fate, however, had doomed their speedy destruction.

The military tactics of the Duke were never so conspicuously displayed as on this great and trying occasion. He had, in fact, suffered the Germans to get into the hollow gully between the two ramparts, not fearing the efforts of the knights of the ram, at least, for some hours, on

* Vide Johnium vel potius Jackium Reevium apud Adelphium extra Templum Barrium, coram Terryetyatesium horis post meridian, post haust, sumpt.

the granite surface of the inner wall, which was built with blocks brought from the Giant's Causeway. It was at his instigation too that the deceitful cry was raised, which seduced the Americans forward. The Yankees, precipitating themselves hastily on the rear of the Germans, occasioned much squeezing and confusion; and while this was at its height, while Sam Rogers was in vain endeavouring to restore order, Sir Gregor Mac. Gregor was sent forward to delude the Jews into that fatal pass. The talent of that great man, and his interest with the Hebrews, soon succeeded. "Sheenies! Sheenies!" cried he, "a fence, a fence!" The cry was sufficient. In a moment the Israelites rushed forward from all quarters, loaded with the trophies of their dexterity, to the supposed place of deposit. A loud rustling of silks and corduroys, flannels and muslins, broadcloth and drugget, felt and beaver, announced their arrival, as, loudly shouting—" Who'll puy, who'll puy?

foivety pe-shent under cosht; traps and toggery, traps and toggery, who'll puy, who'll puy!" they entered the press; while Sir Gregor, with as much adroitness as he displayed at Portobello, evaded them, by climbing up the wall. In a moment the Duke drew up a strong battalion of Jarveys* at the end of the pass, so as to oppose all lateral egress, and by an echelon movement, Sir W. Draper Best, attended by his beloved orderly,† Sergeant Wilde, impanelled a strong array of mounted coal-heavers, hastily summoned for the occasion, on the outer rampart, which was gained without difficulty, as the invaders were all inside; and that distinguished cavalry, armed with pots of porter, sung

* See "The Universal Songster, by Mrs. Hemans."

"Jarvey, Jarvey—here am I, your honour."

† Dr. Toddy is, as usual, in error, when he derives this word from order. See *Transactions of the Court of Common Pleas*—Chapters GOOD HUMOUR and GOOD MANNERS,—*folio* 97, *p.* 742 and 749.

out, " Heavy Wet !" looking with stern defiance
on the entrapped and devoted army below.
The invaders, unable to escape to the right
through the bull-headed knights of the whip,
repelled by the granite towers in front, and
hemmed in behind by Sir William and his coal-
heavers, had turned upon themselves. Jew
fell by the snick-a-snee of the German, and
the jemmy of the Jew, battered out the
brain of the Teutonic warrior. The tomahawk, of Yankee land, descended with fierce
impartiality on the pate of sour-crout or of
sheeny ; and in turn the juvenile crow-bar, or
the shortened sabre of these nations, entered into
the cranium or ripped up the jejunal tripe of
the Americans. No method of escape presented
itself but through the left, and the conclusion
demonstrated the danger of that defile.

Sam did all that man could do, to bring his
army into order. Napoleon at Waterloo, or
Nugent at Cadiz, never did more ; but the hand

of fate was upon him. He was about to ex-
perience God's revenge against punning. The
influx of the Jews alarmed him, and Sir Gregor's
cry led him to remark that "this fence would
ruin his defence." But when he saw the magnificent coal-heavers, led forward by their active chief, "*Quels superbes chevaux !*" he exclaimed, "I am done. Best! Best! thou hast
put me to the worst! Hadst thou been on foot,
I'd have heeded thee not; but now my case is
hopeless, for you are the devil at a charge."

CHAPTER IV.

She died for love, and he for glory.

Miss Mitford.

While this tumultuous spectacle was passing
under the eyes of Harriette, another event, in
which, poor maiden! she had a deeper interest
than the fate of kingdoms or the success of
armies, was going on behind her.

The White Tower was in the rear of the
fortress, which enclosed it on the north, south,
and west. On the east a rock rose perpendicu-
lar and abrupt, to the height of about one hundred and fifty feet, which being supposed not

only impregnable but impassable, was not furnished with any fortifications, except a small
half-moon or ravelin, hastily thrown up by
that gallant prince, John Cade, during his short
though chivalrous reign, and which had now
mouldered into decay. It was therefore deemed
unnecessary, on the one hand, to defend it; on
the other, useless to attempt its attack. We shall
soon see that they were at least in some degree
mistaken.

The mysterious old woman had been, as
indeed all the Merrilies family were, much connected with smugglers; and in former times had
the command of the party which used to supply the soldiery of the Tower with rum and hol-
lands, at reduced prices, and unreduced strength.
In those days, the virtuous Moira, P. T. T. P.
governed the fortress, and he was strict and
severe, having frequently blown smugglers from
the muzzle of the Tower guns, without trial.
It was therefore a hazardous undertaking; but

ingenuity, stimulated by gain, will effect anything.
The idea struck one of the party, a gentleman
of the name of Kiddy Harris, who died of a
pressure on the jugular vein, one fine morning
about eight o'clock, while he was in the act of
admiring the architecture of St. Sepulchre's,
that something might be made of the Impassible
rock, as it was called, and a close investigation
soon proved the correctness of his supposition.

In the middle of the rock; about eighty feet
from the ground, a tree—Heaven knows where
it found the earth to grow from—of considerable dimensions, sprung upwards. By the help
of the newly invented science of aero-pleustics,
or kite-flying,* he succeeded, after various experiments, in fastening a rope to one of the
main branches of the tree, by help of which

---

* Consult Bartholomew Lane, Esq., likewise Nicholas
Alley, Esq, not to mention Corn Hill, Esq., also John
Viscount Glendine, apud Josephum Millerum, p. 41. Vie
Privée, Chap. Agiotage, vol. 7, p. 365.

and the rock itself, Kiddy got up to the oak.
What was his astonishment to find here a cave,
invisible both from above and below, in which
were some mouldering chairs, a table, and instruments of refreshment, the shape of which
denoted them to be of ancient date.   On further
examination he discovered that a flight of steps
had been hollowed up to the base of the tower,
where a small unfenced ledge, of about six feet
wide, projected beyond the building, from which
only it was accessible by a low iron gate, leading
through the guard-room of the Sepoys, into the
area of the fortress.   This platform was rarely
visited ; indeed never but at the annual inspection by the Lord High Constable, escape
or attack on that side being considered, and
with some justice, totally out of the question.
The opening was barely sufficient to admit
one person of moderate dimensions,* and

* Of this a singular proof occurred some time after the
events of which we treat. Mr. Andrews, an eminent book-

no one suspected that it led to any thing.
Through this, Kiddy Harris, Mr. Johnstone,
and the mysterious old woman, who alone were
in the secret, used, on the dark nights of the
new moon, to smuggle in contraband commo-
dities. The male accomplices had long before
this time perished; Kiddy as we have related;
Johnstone in single combat with Sir Hudson
Lowe, who detected him in an attempt to smuggle away his interesting captive in a *chaise percée*
from St. Helena. And it was a long while
since the old woman employed it, because
having been convinced of the impropriety of
smuggling by Mrs. Fry, she had given up the
practice, and commenced the business—in con-
junction with her second paramour (of her first,
anon)—of a receiver of stolen goods. An occa-

seller, who weighed 38 stone, 7lb. 9oz, having attempted
to pass through, stuck in it, and his associates, to save their
own lives and avoid detection, were obliged to cut him in
pieces, which they threw into the Thames, to the great im-
provement of the breed of oysters.

sion came now, however, in which it was necessary for her to return to her ancient bye-path.

The party which left the Clarendon soon
arrived at the Tower by a circuitous route.
They dismounted, and let the horses loose, the
old woman observing that they had no further
use of their services. Two of her pages were
waiting in concealment ; they were a pair of
interesting young natives of the Cambrian prin-
cipality, whom she had nick-named Bubble
and Squeak. She repeated, in a low tone,
chaunting the musical words of the harmonious
Taliesin—

> " Gwrthodi gwrthodes
> Ereill o tylles
> Pan goren gormes
> Yn mhlymwyd maes
> Gorwythawg Gyw-wydd."

To which, a duo of voices replied, one wamb-
ling and bubbling as boiling water over potatoes, the other squeaking in the manner of

a young pig, when some ingenious youth, in
boyish disport, squeezes with pinching finger
its caudal appendage—

> " Trwy iaith ac elfydd
>   Rhitwch rieddawg wydd
> Gantaw yn lluyd
> A rhwyrtran peblig.
> Cad ar llaw annafig."

And as the notes died away, the two youths
were seen creeping on their bellies out of the
hole in which they were hidden. This was the
signal agreed on.

" *Duw fo gyda chwi,*" said the old woman.

" *Duw a'ch bendithio, arglwyddes,*" was the
dutiful reply.

" Taffy," said she to the eldest, " have you
got the ropes and the kites?"

" *Je,*" bubbled the elder mountaineer.

" *Diammau,*" squeaked the younger.

" Proceed then," said she, " with your
operations."

The mountaineers went instantly to work, and Lucy and Cæsar admired the dexterity with which they made their paper bird soar to the oak, as the eagle soars around their native Snowdon. In five minutes their task was accomplished: the rope ladder was firmly fixed to the tree.

" It is done, then, Pendragon ?" asked the woman.

" *Je*," bubbled the first.

"*Diammau*," squeaked the second, as she presented each with a florin, and having promised one some situation about Manchester Buildings, and the other, the high dignity of Grand Goat of the order of St. Cadwallader (in token of which, she stuck a bunch of leeks in his button-hole), she dismissed them. One bubbled out, " *Dyiolwch*"—the other squeaked forth, " *Duw'n rhwydd i chwi*"—and they vanished down an alley. It has never been heard what became of them.

" Up, up," said the old woman ; " Cæsar, you
go first."

" Me feared, Missis,—you go first, Missis,"
said the Ashantee.

" Yes, you rascal," replied the old woman,
" you want to look at my legs, do you?
Whether you see them or not, you shall feel
them"— and suiting the action to the word, as
Harmer, the sheriff's officer, says, she applied her
foot with no small energy to the nether extremity of Cæsar. Against such arguments it
is impossible to reason, and accordingly the
murmuring negro mounted the giddy ascent.
He was followed by the old woman, who occasionally pricked him, when he displayed any
symptoms of fear, or loitering, with Charles
Brandon's spear, which made him advance with
no small degree of velocity. Lucy bearing the
sword, followed, and they reached the tree
without any accident, save the small incon-
venience, which the repeated insertion of the

half-inch of spear blade occasioned to the gluteal organ of Cæsar. On arriving at the cave, the old woman applied to these little orifices, soothing plasters of balmy diachylon, and that being done, drew the rope ladder after her, and the kite to which it was attached. Soon did they ascend the steps, and gain the giddy platform. Lucy was terrified at the dizzy height she had ascended, but " love mastered fear,"* and, with undaunted bosom, she awaited the orders of her mystic guide.

Fortune for a moment seemed against them. The Major, tired of watching in front, came forth to pace upon the projecting ledge, just at the moment the old woman was preparing to hitch the ladder, by means of the kite, on a projecting buttress of the Tower. His first impulse was to start back with astonishment.

" O, by the powers," said he, " what's that ? Are people peeping up out of the could stone

* Sir William Scott, afterwards Lord Towel.

like musharoons, or my friend, Crofty Croker's cluricaunes ? Well, there's no use in talking, we're dished, front and rear, clane done. The Devil and Dr. Foster is agen us. Who are you, in the name of God ?"

" You ought to know me well, Major," replied the old woman, " my blood was near being on your head."

In a moment, he recognised her.

" Ah, then, Mother Solomons, is it you, after all ? Faith, I remember well getting you sentenced to be hanged at the Old Bailey for robbery, in spite of all my friend, Charley Phillips, who gets off more rogues in a month, than any other six of his comrades in a year, and all the illigant swarers you brought out of Petticoat Lane, could do for you, and never did I set my eyes on your ugly mug since you broke prison till this blessed moment."

" Shame be on you, for thus glorying in your persecution of the tender female," replied

Mrs. Solomons; " but your hour is come. Do
you remember what I said ?"

" Much I care about it," was the answer.
" You said, I was to lie dead on the top of an
ould rock under a stone jug.. But —— "
here he perceived Cæsar, who vainly endea-
voured to skulk behind the woman.

" And so you are here too, my purty black
mazzard—yes, faith, nate and genteel you look
in your new wig. I thought I locked you up
snug with my own fore-paws, but the devil is
busy in this Tower to-night. How did you get
out ?"

" There is no use in asking questions," said
the old woman. " Surrender, you are our
prisoner"—and as she spoke, she sprung forward, snapt the key of the iron gate out of his
hand, turned it in the creaking wards, and then
flung the instrument clean over the precipice.

The Major, disconcerted as he was, and cut

off from his Sepoys, soon, however, recovered his native intrepidity.

" Surrender ! no, ma'am, thank you ! It shall never be said, that I surrendered to an old fence, a black ruffian, and a girl. No, faith, you are *my* prisoners, and I advise you to submit in pace."

With a solemn air the old woman turned to Lucy. " *Now is the time !* Unsheath the sword of Courcy."

" O blood and fire !" exclaimed the Major, " here's the people the Duke wants. Surrender, I say, you robbing vagabones. I say, surrender in the King's name."

She paid no attention, but proceeded :

" Unsheath the sword of Courcy, and slay the jailor of your love."

At the word, an expressible enthusiam seized on the beauteous maid. She unsheathed the glittering faulchion, and exclaimed—

" Whoever thou art, O man, surrender!
Let not thy blood be on my blade, thy grey
hairs upon its haft. I give you quarter if you
submit to be bound."

" Bound! I never was bound but once, and
that was in £50 myself, and two recognizances
in £25 each, to keep the pace against a young
jack-a-dandy, whose head I broke for im-
pertinence, and you're no trading justice, I
fancy."

" Again, I say, submit. Trifle not with thy
life."

" Is it in airnest, you are, my darling girl.
Do you think, I'd lift a hand agen a lady? God
forbid!"

" Prepare, then," she said, with a solemn
tone, " prepare, unhappy man, to die," and she
lifted the sword.

" So it must be done, after all! O, murther
—murther—that my father's son should ever
raise his arm against a girl, except to take the

jewel round the waist and give her a dozen
kisses. Well, I won't hurt the cratur, if I
can help it. Come out." said he, " tickle-
gizzard," drawing his cut-and-thrust, " come
out, my old joker—ashamed you are, poor fellow, that you who was never afeared of a man,
should, after thirty years' fighting, be lugged
out against a woman."

With these words, the reluctant soldier began
this strange contest. The strength and practice
of the Major, was a counterbalance to the
superior instrument of the girl, and the combat
much resembled that which takes place at the
conclusion of the war of Abrahamides.* He
ducked beneath her two handed blows—while
the length of her weapon made his thrusts
unavailing, or, if by chance a hit took place, it
glanced harmless from her impenetrable armour.
Fire flashed from the blades and the eyes of
both, and feats of dexterity, agility, and skill

* Vide Quadrupeds, Act II. scen. ult.

were performed, which, when we consider the
narrow stage on which they took place, would
have done honour to an O'Shaughnessy. At
last, however, she was evidently becoming
wearied—which, considering the weight of her
sword and armour, is not to be wondered at
—when the old woman, watching her opportunity, when the Major's back was turned,
slipped one of the ropes of her ladder through
his arms, and effectually retained him, while
Lucy, rushing forward, ran the sword through
his body up to the hilt, wounding Cæsar, who
stood too close behind, slightly in the abdomen.
" Me no luck to-night," growled the unreasonable negro, in one of those sulky fits, which
blacks occasionally take; but there was no time
to notice *him*.

" That will do, darling," said the dying Ma-
jor, "give yourself no more trouble about it.
That's a thrust which would puzzle the pope.
You have managed your tooth-pick in style.

Believe the word of an ould soldier, I'm done—
going to God with a fair wind at my tail. I
don't envy your husband the luck of getting
you, my purty posy ; faith, he'll have no joke
in keeping you quiet."

Lucy, awe-struck with what she had done, was
mute. The old woman, however, addressed the
dying Major :—

" Is not my prophecy true, hapless man?
Rememberest thou not my words of might ?

> 'On a cold rock you will lie so snug,
> Perched at the foot of an old stone jug.'

" No, faith," said the expiring man, " I never
stuffed such rubbish into my head, having no
taste for poetry. Lave me die in pace. I wonder, do I remember e'er a prayer at all."

At the word prayer, the religious feelings
of Cæsar, who occasionally assisted his master
in preaching, were roused, and forgetful of his
wound, which he stuffed with a piece of oakum,

he happened to have in his pocket, came forward, and taking a hymn-book from his breast, approached the Major.

"Oh, Massa," said he, "Massa, you bad Massa, you be in de first page of black book. 'Massa Major, for wicked Massa,' de debil write it wid him own big paw. O, Massa, sing dis hymn wid me. My own good Massa, him was hanged, write it himself. Him is hymn dirty. Tickler measure.

> " ' When de wicked buckra die,
> Debil him is standy by,
> Wid a fire in him big eye
>   And a tal, lal, la!
> Did him drink too much sangree,
> Wid de girls him make too free.'

But you no sing, Massa?"

"Sing!" said the Major, whose spirit was fast departing; "sing! I wish I was well for five minutes, and I'd make *you* sing at the wrong side of your mouth. Why, you noisy

scoundrel, if you had as much religion in you
as a rat, you would not be singing anthems
over me, like a cock-raven, but would give me
something to drink." His mind here wandered.
" Ha !" said he,—" the fight—the Tower—in
flames—in water—the rush of steeds."—Reason
returned for a moment.

" I say," said he, " you mangy mullott, if
you were any good, you would bring me a
glass of grog, cold, without water."

Madness again predominated.

' " The war rages. Who is that on the grey
horse ? Slay him. Smite him down. Put me
in the thick of the fight, among the clash of
spears. Where is my hauberk ? gird on my
morrion. Ha—do you fly ?—On, cowards, on to
the breach. Huzza, huzza ! They run, they
run !"

Here another glimpse of reason flashed upon
his mind.

" I die an honest ould Protestant; in pace

with all mankind, barring my inimies, and
them I hope the devil will soon have by the
back of the poll. As for you, Master Sazer,
I give you one hint, which is this; you'll
be hanged, my fine fellow, by the neck, and
that soon. I wish I had a dro —— "

"Drop," he would have said, but the rattles
of death split the P, and cut off the " drink,"
that was intended to follow. He did not die
unrevenged, in some measure; for just before
his dying moment, he flung with his remaining
strength his sword at Mrs. Solomons; it pierced
her side, and she immediately fainted on the
platform. Lucy, almost distracted, was near
fainting herself, when the old woman suddenly
revived.

"It was doomed," she faintly said; "I am
here to die. But an hour is given me, and in
that hour I have much to do."

She then calmly bound up her wounds, and
proceeded with her task as if nothing had oc-

curred. Her grieved companions assisted her in her labours, and ere long the kite had fastened the ladder to the top of the White Tower. With hasty step they ascended, and soon stood before the astonished Harriette, just at the moment she asked the question as to the disappearance of the Jews. It was not easy, however, to disconcert Harriette.

" O, *mon Dieu !*" she exclaimed, " *comme cela est bien drole*. How is this?"

" Fair Harriette," said Mrs. Solomons, " we have no leisure now to explain. You shall know in due time. Where is Mr. Smithers ?"

" Below," she answered, " in the topmost donjon."

" Let us then descend to him without delay ; we come to free him and you."

" *Je vous remercie, ma chere ;* but so odd a figure, I never ———"

" No words," said the peremptory matron.

Awed into submission, Harriette sprung

down, and the whole party followed.   Who
can paint the emotion of Smithers ?   Astonishment at the descent as it were from the clouds
—wonderment at the strange condition of Cæsar
—amazement at the sibylline figure of the hag,
occupied his mind in an instant.   But all other
feelings were swallowed up when he recognized
his love.   He asked not how she came ; he offered no conjecture as to her warlike gear—her
blood-stained sword ; he inquired not as to
her strange attendant ; he sympathised not
with his bemauled slave ; there *she* stood, the
idol of his affections—the treasured vision of
his soul, and all else was forgotten.   In a transport of joy he clasped her in his arms, he pressed
her yielding lips to his, he strained her in a close
and rapturous embrace.   What were at such
a moment to him or to her, the chilly forms of
society, the damping decrees of decorum ?
Nothing.

The old woman, who gazed upon him with

intense affection, permitted the lovers a few
minutes of enjoyment. She herself had once
loved, and she now felt for others. Cæsar, forgetting his wounds, danced around in an agony
of joy. But there was another in the dungeon,
to whom the sight brought any thing but hap-
piness. It was the hapless Harriette. Rage,
first, then grief, took possession of her soul.
She seized the whinyard of John de Courcy,
which Lucy had dropped in the ardour of her
embrace, and at first lifted it to smite her rival,
ay, and even her lovely mulatto. But this
was no more than a momentary fit; calmer
thoughts succeeded, and the silent tear trickled
down her pallid cheek. Unnoticed by the rest,
she gazed with a transport of despair, on the
entwined lovers.

"What!" thought she, in this her altered
mood; "slay *him!* Shed the blood of him on
whom I doat with a devoted attachment! O!
wicked woman, to suffer such an idea to cross

your mind, even for a second. Slay her! no, no; too blessed woman, your life is safe. Why should I render *him* unhappy, why deprive him of the object on which his affections are placed? Live, then, fortunate rival. I will not entail misery on him, for whom I could willingly die. *Die!* Happy thought, and for him I *will* die, and that this moment."

Such were the tender yet desperate sentiments of Harriette. Her current of thought, indeed, was habituated to run in the most refined and delicate channel.

She stepped among the group, with a firm though hurried step. A maniac wildness was in her eye, while the calm determination on death, had stamped a rigid energy on her features, now paler than the snows of Caucasus. She leant upon De Courcy's sword. The whole would have been a groupe for Raphael or Theodore Lane. The lovers started asunder; the old woman leant in silence against the wall, and

Cæsar, squatting in the manner of the Asia-
tics, and Mr. Place, of Charing Cross, scratch-
ing his head, awaited the result with open
mouth.

" A moment," exclaimed Harriette, " but a
moment! I shall not intrude longer on your
transports. Smithers, it was a fatal hour that
threw thee in my way. Fleeting affections had
till then crossed my heart; but love, burning,
glowing, irrepressible love—never before. I
thought that my charms—I may speak of them
now — charms which royalty had flattered,
which had been the toast of a hundred nobles,
might have won your affection. I hoped also
that the service which I could render you,
would have wrought upon you ——"

" Generous woman !" exclaimed Smithers.
"I—— "

" Be silent, beloved of my soul, and hear me
to the end. I thought I might have enlisted
your affections through your gratitude, and my

day-dreams wove many a fairy scene of bliss,
now melted into nothing."

She burst into tears. Smithers stammered
a few words of consolation; Lucy had recourse
to her smelling bottle, and the old woman to
her snuff-box; and Cæsar, dropping his lower
jaw still deeper, scratched his head with a more
rapid motion. She soon recovered, and resumed:

"It is done; Madam, may you be happy;
allow me one kiss from your love. One, only one."

Lucy could not speak; she bowed assent. Smithers pressed the cold lip of the girl in silence.

"When I lie in death," she continued,
"think of me, as one who loved not wisely,
but too well. Thus—then—thus—thus!"

A cry of horror burst from all, and they
rushed forward to prevent the rash purpose,
but in vain. With the rapidity of lightning
she had thrice plunged the sword in her breast,

and her crimson blood distained her ivory bosom. She died almost in a moment. Her last words were — " John Joseph—Jeremy John ——" Her last look was on the beauteous eye of Smithers, and in a moment her chaste soul fled to her Creator.

A mournful silence ensued, which Mrs. Solomons broke.

"We have no time now," said she, "for grief. Poor girl! I knew her when Lord Pon—— but no matter!"

Lucy shed a tear over her hapless rival, and Smithers bit his lip, without saying a word.

" Up, Cæsar," said the old woman, " up, rascal, we must make you our step-ladder."

It was in vain for Cæsar to refuse, so first his master, then the old woman, then Lucy, used his shoulders to get upon the summit of the Tower. When there, they deliberated as to what was to be done with Cæsar. The old woman proposed leaving him there; for she argued he might as well be hanged then, as at any other time, and hanged infallibly he would be, when the Duke discovered him with the dead body of Harriette. All the water in the Thames, she said, would not save him. Lucy was neutral, but Smithers pleaded for his faithful slave. Cæsar's supplications were loud, "He feared the ghost of the dead Missis," he said, and howled with agony. At last the old woman relented, and lowering a rope, which he fastened under his arm-pits, she pulled him up, with no farther harm than a slight dislocation of the shoulder.

CHAPTER V.

At fault !—Remit your eager speed,
　Draw up the tightened rein ;
Breathe, breathe awhile the impetuous steed,
　His furious course restrain.
Another view !—Halloo !—Again then we fly,
And the speed of our high-mettled coursers we'try ;
　　Again ply the whistling lash,
　　Again through the torrent we dash,
　　　Down the vale sweep,
　　　Climb up the steep,
　　　O'er the wall leap.
　　　　Tally-ho !

　　　　　　MRS. HANNAH MORE.

Woo'd and married and a',
Woo'd and married and a' ;
　And isn't she very well off
Who's woo'd and married and a' ?

　　　　　　MISS EDGEWORTH.

THEY descended from the top of the Tower
to the platform below, where Smithers noticed,
with a grim smile, the stiff and stark body of

his enemy, the Major, and pressed to his heart the hand that did the deed.   Thence they reached the cave, where the old woman lay down quite exhausted on the stone floor.

" God bless you, my children," she said ; " I have done my business in this world, and my hour is come.   John Jeremy, come hither, my beloved, and receive the dying benediction of your grandmother."

" My grandmother !" said Smithers, with astonishment. — " Venerated dame, do you speak in earnest ?"

" Look here," said she, drawing a lock of curly red hair from her bosom, " this is one of the first locks cut from your father's head."

" The colour certainly corresponds," said our hero.

" He had the mark of an anchor burnt in with gunpowder on his left arm, just under the variolous cicatrice ?"

" 'Tis true."

" On his right foot there were but four toes—
a natural defect ?"

"; You speak the fact."

" Nay, more—read this letter."

She handed a rumpled note to our hero, who
read it with profound reverence. It ran thus:

" ONURD MOTHER,

" This fu lines to let you no Ime live an well
thanks be to Godd for the sem. Has got a
good berth abord the Praisegodbarebones belonging to a quaker hows in Livrpool, and Nu
York, of the name o Shovel and Slateface, and
is bound to the cost of Africa to snap niggars
—of wich cattle there's much want now in the
West Ingies.

" If you cud no anny ship goin to Benny or
Annamaboo, you mite find a sailor to take me
sum shurts, an if you cud rise a five poun note,

so much the better. But don't trubble yourself about munny only they shirts wud be convenyent, for cleen linnen is cumfortable here.

"Hopping youre well as Ime at this present riting.

"I remane

"Yr jewtiful sun

"till deth

"Izzy Smithers.

"*On bord the Praisegodbarcbones.*

"*New York Harbor.*

"*July 4th,* 1799.

"Libberty for ever. Huzza!"

It was directed—

"To my mother

"Mrs. Israel Solomons

"Petticoat Lane

"in

"London

"England."

"Yes," said Smithers, visibly affected by this interesting document, "it is his! The style, the manly sentiments, the peculiar orthography denote the work of Isaac Smithers, my honoured sire. It was on that voyage he kidnapped my mother, beloved woman. What feelings does not this call up. Shovel and Slateface! Often have I heard him speak of these venerable men. They it was, who, when the Slave Trade was abolished, were so much struck by its horrors, as to raise so potent a cry against it in both hemispheres. To them, too, is the religious bias of my father's mind in his subsequent life to be attributed. To them his pious career in the West Indies, until it was cut off by the rope of the British hangman! But I must not forget my grandmother."

He fell immediately on his knees before her, and she pronounced her avial benediction. Tears flowed from the eyes of Lucy at this touching spectacle. When the agitation of the party had somewhat subsided, the old woman continued :

" My story is brief. Of gipsy descent, my early life was spent in wandering with my tribe, which, when I was about fifteen, got into trouble, and was obliged to disperse. I steered, in company with an elder matron, for Wapping, where I fell a victim to the attractive arts, (and three guineas,) of a captain of a collier, whose name I now forget. After remaining with him for about a fortnight, he left me, and I never saw him again. In about four months after, during which time I picked up a precarious existence, my shape denoted that I was destined at that early age soon to become a mother. My charms at this period attracted the eye of Mr. Timothy Smithers, who kept a shop for marine stores, at the corner of Bull Alley, Ratcliffe Highway, and under his roof your father was born."

" I shall not fail to visit the hallowed spot," said Smithers, gasping with emotion.

" Mr. Smithers took the child as his own, and baptized him Isaac, in compliment to an out-partner of his, Mr. Isaac, commonly called Mr. Izzy Lazarus. Your grandfather, as I may style him, was a class-leader in the methodist connection, and his picture is to be found in one of the volumes of the Methodist Magazine."

" Which volume?" eagerly demanded the hero of our tale.

" I forget," she replied, " but I think the thirteenth. His hair was straight and sleek, and his countenance soapy. With him I lived many years, until his dealings attracted the notice of the avaricious magistrates, and the arbitrary order of the ruthless Sir John Sylvester, con-signed him to the House of Correction, in which horrid dungeon he died."

" Horrible government !" exclaimed Smithers, " no wonder that you are hastening to your fall !"

" I then took up with Mr. Israel Solomons, and embraced the Jewish faith. Ikey, dear, darling Ikey, now in North America, is my son. He has been torn from these aged arms. He was the brother of your sainted father. Alas ! that my son, the missionary, and my son, the receiver, should both be victims of tyrannous oppression, and both with equal injustice."

Smithers gnashed his teeth with rage and defiance ; and the old woman, in a pensive tone, continued the adventures of her interesting family. .

" Your father, always wild, got among some gay companions, the consequences of which led him into the presence of the Lord Mayor, when he was about twelve years old. It was something about a pocket handkerchief. The war was going on, and sailors were wanting, so his Lordship let him off on condition he went to sea, and he was obliged to go cabin-boy on board the Thunder. Bomb. ordered to cruise in the West Indies. Being a clever fellow, he contrived, in two or three years, to desert, got into the American merchant service, and was much employed in the slave business until that was done up. He then came to London, where his father's fame among the methodists introduced him to the chief people of their church, and his knowledge of the West Indies pointed him out as the proper missionary for a new society, there established. You know the rest. He preached liberty, and —— died."

"A deed of horror, still to be avenged!" cried Smithers. "But proceed. All this is new to me: and it serves to explain many dark mysteries in my life."

"After the death of old Mr. Solomons, my son's wife managed the business, and I took to fortune-telling, and magic arts. By these means I have obtained, like most people in my condition, unbounded power. I was determined to free you."

" How did you know me ?"

She smiled, in conscious pride of art.

" There was not a tobacco smuggler from
Barbadoes who did not bring me tidings of
your movements, and I knew the precise time
you were to land. I knew the motives that
took you to Dover, and accordingly had all the
Dover coachees on the alert. From them I
learnt the coach in which you were to come,
and I witnessed your first meeting with this
lovely maid. A coal-heaver in Hungerford
Market, with whom I was taking a pot of stout
last night, told me he had seen you—he did not
know it was you, but he described your person
—taken to the Tower. I had the whole plan
at once arranged. I drew upon the chest of
one of my tribes—for I still keep up the gipsy,
the methodist, and the Jewish connection—for
money. I hired and disposed my agents. I
retraced my old paths. I brought you together
—Lucy, you remember my prediction—I have

freed you—I have seen the Major slain—and
I die.   Take this purse (she gave him a wallet,
containing a bunch of keys), you will find written directions how to use it.   I die happy—
fly through —— "

  Her voice failed—she was convulsed—her eye
became fixed,—her features rigid—and, uttering
a deep groan, she was no more.

  " Alas !" said Smithers, " no sooner found
than lost.   A mausoleum shall shroud thy
bones, but time presses now, and I cannot pay
your remains the honours which they deserve."

  He kissed her dead lips, and Cæsar having
arranged the rope-ladder, they gained the
ground and liberty once more.   Lucy here
divested herself of her cumbrous armour, and
they determined on returning before their flight
could be discovered.   But where were they to
go ?   Smithers or Cæsar knew nothing of
London, and Miss Hawkins had never been so
far east before.

"Perhaps," said Smithers, "my grandmother may have cared for this. Let me examine her papers."

He found his supposition correct, for, on opening the packet, he saw written at the top of the first paper—

"FLY THROUGH THE TUNNEL."

"The Tunnel!" said Smithers.

"The Tunnel!!" said Lucy.

"De Dunnel!!!" said Cæsar.

A gentleman of the name of Beamish, passing by, caught the word.

"Sir," said he to Smithers, "I see that you are a stranger. The Tunnel lies this way—wast curosity—werry. Show it to gemmen and ladies, one shilling—servants, tradesmen, and children, half price. This way, gemmen, this way. Follow me."

Following this obsequious person, they soon arrived at the Tunnel, which had just been carried under the Thames. Lofty columns of

porphyry supported a roof of alabaster, from
which swung ten thousand cressets, fed with
naphtha and asphaltus, "yielding light as from
a sky." Its gates were of solid silver, and the
pavement within, Parian marble, of dazzling
hue. Above, the Thames played in murmuring eddies, and it was warmed from below by
the central fire kindled by the ingenious Hut-
ton. It is in vain to seek for it now. When
Smithers approached, its hours were numbered.
Astonished as he was at the splendour of the
scene, he did not forget the purpose of his visit.
Thanking his guide for his civility, and com-
plimenting him with a douceur of five shillings,
he passed through this greatest of bores, with
hasty step. On emerging into upper air, a
sound of horns and a cry of hounds burst on
the astonished ears of the emancipated trio; and,
turning to see whence it came, they perceived
a gallant company of huntsmen scouring through
an open lawn, in a spacious forest, on the left.

" Ho—ho—tantivy !"—" Yoicks, yoicks!"—
" Hark forward !"—and other expressions of the
chase, rung on all sides. Smithers had arrived
most opportunely. A chivalrous-looking knight,
with wisdom stamped upon his brow, had been
thrown from his horse, and was attacked by an
infuriated boar, the object of their chase. Grunt-
ing with rage, his jaws covered with foam, he ran
furiously at the cavalier ; when Smithers, with
the celerity of thought, boldly threw himself
between the unhorsed huntsman and his savage
foe. Seizing the beast by his long tusks, he called
aloud to Lucy, who immediately snatched a
boar-spear from one of the attendants, and, with
.matchless dexterity and strength, transfixed the
heart of the monster. He bounded several feet
from the ground, on receiving his *coup de grace*,
overturning Cæsar, who was close behind his
master in the action, and inflicting a compound
fracture of the right patella. The cavalier
having recovered from his alarm, thanked

Smithers in a most gracious manner, which
induced him, after having consulted Cæsar, and
Lucy, to throw himself upon the mercy of the
knight.

"Great prince," said he, approaching, "for
though I know you not, such your aspect be-
speaks you —— "

"He is a witch, Colonel," said the person
thus addressed," a'n't he?—ha! ha! ha!"

"Your Royal Highness makes yourself
known, by your noble presence, wherever you
are seen," replied the bowing equerry.

"Do I then address a prince of the blood?"
asked Smithers.

"You have the honour, Sir," said the Colonel, "of addressing his Royal Highness the
Duke of Gloucester."

Smithers lost no time in dropping upon his
bended knee.

"Fortunate that I am in having to plead my
cause before such a tribunal."

" A—what !" said the Duke.

" He means a judge, please your Royal Highness," responded the equerry.

" Why don't he say then what he means ?" said the Duke. " Talk plain language, man, not like the words they put in books to puzzle people."

Smithers, complying with the advice of the Duke, who, open-mouthed, was inhaling the balmy breezes of morning, made his story plain to the meanest capacity.

We need not tell our readers, what they know already. He denied any participation in the insurrections raised every where against England—repeated that he sought for justice by constitutional means only—protested his innocence of any charge that could be made against him, and declared he knew not for what he had been confined—alluded delicately to the fate of Harriette—and blushingly hinted at the

interest which he took in his fair companion.
The Duke comprehended the most of the story,
without much difficulty, with the aid of his
equerry, and declared his intention to protect
the innocent and brave.

"I'll take care of the Admiralty for you,
Mr. a—a—a—what's your name?"

"Smithers, please your Royal Highness."

"Well, Mr. Smithers, I'll save you from the
Admiralty.   They carry things there in a—
what d'ye call it — you know what I mean,
Colonel."

"Your Royal Highness is pleased to mean,
that they carry on affairs at the Admiralty in
an arbitrary manner," said the equerry.

"Precisely so, that's what I meant, precisely," said the Duke.   "Mr. Smithers, you're
safe."

Our hero bowed in gratitude.

"But, though free from the bonds of the
Tower, you are still in those of Mercury."

" His Royal Highness," said the equerry to Smithers, " means to say, Venus."

" Yes, yes," said the Duke, " Venus—and would have no objection to be in those of — you know what I mean, Colonel."

" Your Royal Highness," said the equerry, " is pleased to mean Hymen."

The lovers did not speak, but their blushes assented.

" Come then," said the Duke, " as the man in the play says of a beef-steak, when 'tis to be done, let it be done quickly. We have the Chishop of Bitchester—Bishop of Chichester, I mean—here with us at this hunt, and a hard-riding dog he is. Hola, Bishop !"

The portly prelate rode up on his sorrel charger, and, bare-headed, awaited the orders of the prince.

" Go back to the palace," said he, " and put your traps in order. Here is a pair of culprits waiting to be chained. Ha! ha! ha! I don't

mean really chained—I was only joking; ha!
ha! ha!"

"Ha! ha! ha!" said the Colonel.

"Ha! ha! ha!" said the Page.

"Ha! ha! ha!" said the Bishop.

"Devilish good—vastly smart—getting better
every day," &c. &c. &c., said every body.

"I only meant that they wanted to be married," continued the Duke, "and you are the
man.   So get all ready."

"D—d hard this," growled the departing
Bishop.   "Such a morning, and the scent
lying so divinely.   D—me but I'm in a better
humour for uncoupling than for coupling.   But
pocas palabras.   Here I go."

The bliss of our lovers may be more easily con-
ceived than described, and we shall not therefore
undertake the task.   They prepared to follow the
Bishop, when the attention of all was turned away
from every thing else, by a cry of unparalleled
agony, which seemed to issue from the bottom of

the river. So dire a cry never burst upon
human ear. Every eye looked towards the stream,
and, there a scene of wonder was before them.
It seemed as if a convulsion had taken place, for
its bosom was heaving and swelling with un-
wonted throes. On the topmost eddy whirled,
round and round, a cock-boat, containing two
persons, who laboured might and main to escape
from the infuriated waters. In a moment all
was smooth again, but the boat was gone. A
hundred yachts were immediately launched, to
endeavour to save the devoted passengers, when
it suddenly submerged from the waters, and
made towards the shore where the Ducal party
was standing. As it neared the land, the cock-
swain was discovered to be Lord Goderich, and
his companion the Duke of Wellington. Cæsar
and his master intuitively hid themselves behind a tree. " Aye," said Lord Goderich, on
landing—" Aye, choke the scoundrels, they

are done, I fancy. Pretty considerably water-
logged, the ruffians. Devil sweep'em."

"Amen!" responded the Duke; "but I am
wet through and through. Whom have we
here? Ah! Gloucester, my boy, give us the
fist."

His Royal Highness, who had not heard, except vaguely, from Smithers, any thing of the
attack, naturally inquired of the Duke an
account of the strange sight he had seen, and
his Grace detailed to him what he knew. We
take up the story where we left it.

When, by the manœuvring of the Duke, the
whole of the attacking army was hemmed up
in the defile between the two ramparts, and had
no way of escape—victory was now hopeless—
but, laterally, to the right, to their great astonishment and joy, the gate which kept them in on
that quarter was opened; it was a part of the
Duke's stratagem. The devoted host rushed

blindly through this pass, this whole Ducal army
urging them in the rear, through a winding defile, where many a life was lost in their hasty retreat. This passage led to the Tunnel, and into
that deadly hollow the fugitives fled pell-mell.
The Duke was prepared for this, and while
Smithers was in conversation with his Royal
Highness, Brunel and Beamish, with five hundred masons, had passed over, and in a few
minutes built up an impenetrable wall at the
further end. The silver gates were closed at the
near end; and, by cutting off the pipes that conveyed the gaseous naphtha, the wretched invaders
were in total darkness. The Tunnel was her-
metically sealed, and escape was impossible..

Many perished by the hands of their friends—
others were trod to death; but the remainder
was not destined long to continue alive.

" Five hundred pounds," said the Duke,
" to any man, who will go in a boat and pull

U

out the central plug of the Tunnel, and let in the water on these villains."

No one answered, for it was evident that the man who attempted it would do so at the hazard of his life. After a pause, the Duke said, " he would go for one, but who will steer ?"

. " I," said Lord Goderich, " I. I do not think I was born to be drowned."

" Valiant man," said the Duke, and embraced him in front of the army. A life-boat was instantly launched. Lord Goderich took the helm, and the Duke, pulling a pair of sculls, came to the spot where the existence of the plug was indicated by a buoy, surmounted by a flag. Why conceal the fact ? Iron as were the nerves of the Lord High Constable, he hesitated for a moment ; but at last, saying something about Curtius, he seized the ring of the plug, and, exerting all his strength, tore up the key-stone of the arch. A mighty gush of waters followed—a cry of agony and despair rung from the wretched inmates of the Tunnel, and affrighted the very birds. In a minute the tunnel was full, and, in another minute, Jew, German, and American had ceased to exist. In a century afterwards, their bones were gathered into a catacomb, with an inscription in heroic verse, from the classical pen of Professor Millman :—

> Reader, you here behold the bones,
> Of people gone to Davy Jones.
> 'Neath father Thames's whelming tide,
> Poor rogues! like puppies blind, they died.
> Out of the bore by Brunel dug,
> Duke Wellington he pulled the plug,
> And drowned the tottle, of them snug.

The Duke related his exploit with glowing satisfaction. "I am so happy," said he, "that whatever boon is asked of me, I shall grant."

"I ask, then," said he of Gloucester.

"I grant before hand," replied Wellington.

"Come forth," said he, "Smithers, from your hiding place. I ask your Grace's pardon for these culprits, who have been so unlucky as to offend you."

Smithers and the trembling Cæsar advanced.

" So ho !" said Lord Goderich, " so ho ! you ugly vagabond, how did you steal away ? By ——"

" Silence, Goderich," said his Grace. " My word is passed, and these wretches are pardoned ; though you know not, Sir," turning gravely to Gloucester, " what you have asked. Mr. Smithers, who is that young lady with you ?"

" A lady," said Smithers, " who is about to unite her fortunes, for good and evil, with mine."

The Duke's brow brightened somewhat.

" Is Harriette then a companion of your flight ?"

" Pardon the unwilling messenger of evil, your Grace," said Smithers, " Harriette is with the angels."

" Dead, villain ?" said the Duke, " dead ! Poor Harriette dead, by *your* hands   Say so, and no power on earth saves you from being torn by wild horses."

" He looks like a murderer," said Goderich ; if I were you, I would not bother myself looking for any proof, but tear him on the spot. Have you any unbroken horses, Gloucester ?"

" My Lord," said Smithers, " if you knew me, you would not speak of me thus. As Heaven is my witness, I did my utmost to prevent the sad deed. She died by her own act."

His Grace covered his eyes with the back of his bony hand, and wept aloud. The triumph of victory, the extinction of his foes, the glory of the morning, was all forgotten. She was dead, and the heaven of his life, was deprived for ever of its sun.

" This lady, and my servant, and a woman since dead, could testify," continued Smithers, " the truth of my assertion."

" Pretty evidence, indeed," said Goderich ; " your wife's testimony you know cannot be received in your case ; and, of the other two, one is dead, and the other, that black savage, who would swear away the life of his father, for a mouthful of molasses.

" Nay, Goderich," said his grace, who had somewhat recovered, " let us examine into the affair quietly. Young man, tell your story. If you vary from the truth, your blood be upon your head."

Smithers, protesting his veracity, related what the reader already knows. The Duke muffled his head in his cloak, and groaned heavily amid the sympathizing group.

" Your story, young man," said he, when it was concluded, " wears such an air of probability that I believe it; it is like poor Harriette," and he wiped his eyes. " And my brave Major too. If I find, on examination, things in the situation you describe, you are secure; but never come into my sight again. There is no resisting the hand of Fate. It was

doomed that this was to be so ;" and solemnly
looking up to Heaven, he added, " *Fiat volun-
tas tua.* Come, Goderich, to our boat. The
sight of this gaiety saddens my soul."

" Well," said Goderich, " if I had my way,
that villain —— "

" Waste not words—my resolution is taken :
—Gloucester, adieu !"

He waived his hand to the crowd, who accompanied him in reverential silence ; and the
boat being rowed by six of the stoutest pullers
of the neighbourhood, soon conveyed its melancholy burthen to the fortress. A rapturous
greeting awaited the victorious warrior ; but the
astonished soldiery were received with a harsh
order to be silent. He went to the White
Tower, where, without uttering a word, he
kissed the cold, but still lovely lips of Harriette,
and, by a motion of his arm, ordered her to be
conveyed into his palace. Descending, he shook
the hand of the dead Major, and had him re-

moved. Having examined the passage to the cave, and found the old woman's body, of which he did not appear to take the slightest notice, he had the oak cut down, and the passage stopped. In some twenty years afterwards, when the affair was forgotten, it was opened by chance, and the bones of the old woman being discovered, it gave the Earl of Aberdeen an opportunity of writing a paper for the Antiquarian Society, to prove that they were those of Fair Rosamond, whose cave he, by ingenious argument, demonstrated it to be. Her skeleton was put in the museum of the Antiquarians. The Major was buried with military honours in Westminster Abbey, among the ruins of which the celebrated inscription, written by Pierce Egan, is still to be seen ; and a stately monument covered the remains of Harriette in St. James's Square. It has long since been destroyed.

On the other side of the river the festivities

"Ods fiddles and flutes," said the Duke, "why should we look so mournful. Let us be —curse on these blue-bottles, they are always flying down my mouth—let us be gay."

With these words he gave Lucy his arm, and proceeded to the palace, where the Bishop of Chichester having performed his office, she became the bride of the too happy Smithers; and the prelate and the bridegroom, having executed Wordsworth's difficult duet of

> Happy tawney Moor!* Happy tawney Moor!
> Wont you, love,
> Waltz a little with your true love;
> Wont you, by the way,
> Hear the bag-pipes play,
> With their chanters gay,
> Squeaking, Johnny, follow now your spouse so bonny;
> Squeak a squeak,
> Squeak a squeak,
> &c. &c. &c,
> *Da Capo.*

the interesting ceremony concluded.

* Not Tommy Moore, as pronounced by some illiterate dillettanti.

CHAPTER VI.

Apollo and Mercurius and the rest.

WILLIAM CORNWALL BARRY PROCTER,
ATTORNEY AT LAW.

THE important affair having thus terminated,
our hero rushed, like a whirlwind, into the arms
of love: the echo of the nuptial kiss was heard
far around ; and His Royal Highness, while
the tear of general sympathy rolled slow and
solemn adown his manly cheek, was preparing
to quit a scene, which, as a perhaps over-scru-
pulous delicacy suggested, the presence even of
the most venerated by-stander might unseason-
ably embarrass.

Smithers observed what was passing in the princely mind, and in an instant was recalled to a proper sense of what he owed to himself, to his love, and to his fame. " No," thought he, " it shall not be said hereafter, that Smithers was unable to bear the cup of bliss to his lips with a steady hand !"

An expedient immediately presented itself to his ever fertile imagination : an hour (he calcu- lated) must elapse ere breakfast could be ready : how to pass that yawning interval—that seem- ing eternity—that never terminating void ?— " Yes," said the hero, I have it. They will say I am mad—crazy—insane—quixotic—de- lirious ! What then ?—Posterity will do me justice !"

" May it please your Highness —— "

" Royal Highness, if it like thee," quoth Gloucester.

" I crave your grace," replied Smithers, and proceeded—" will your Royal Highness have

the condescension to take care of Mrs. S., for a
few minutes? I have been direfully exhausted
—body and mind, in mutual grinding of re-action,
have partly succumbed—I feel sick—faint—"

" Help! help, my good Lord!" cried the
ever sensitive bride—" help, or he dies—."

" Nay, jewel of my soul, let not thy fears,
sweet maiden, conquer the firmness of thy
judicious mind," whispered Smithers; " I am
well; I did but feign, in order not to offend
the Duke. The truth is, my sainted father en-
joined me ever to return thanks to the Divine
Being in private, when blessings such as this
have been vouchsafed. Would you, my Lucy,
break in upon the demands of filial duty, of
religious piety? Suffer me to retire. Speedily
shall I return to press to my lips, the lips which
are dearer to me than the light of heaven."

He put his hand between hers. It was, as
Sir Walter Scott expressed it on another occasion, ' ebon alternate and ivory.'

" O fie! O fie! my Smithers," sighed the agitated maid, and she averted her blushes. " But go, go and indulge your pious propensities. Go, I enjoin you."

He smiled: that smile conveyed more fully than ten volumes could ever do, the grace and the dignity of that noble mind.

" Adieu! for a moment, adieu," said he, "sweet maid.—Illustrious prince, deign to forgive me—where, after all, could I leave beauty so safely as in the custody of wisdom?"

" Come, Smithers," said the Duke, " no fine speeches: if you must go, you must; and I have always heard, and believe it, that when you are there, you cannot be here, and when you are here, you cannot be there—at least so the colonel told me, and I never found him out in a lie yet."

Smithers knew etiquette too well to defer complying with the distinct mandate of royalty; so, retreating, with his face towards the prince until he reached the corner, he disappeared; and pursuing his onward course with his usual locomotive velocity, kept a sharp outlook among the sign-posts, resolved to turn into the first tap-room which should happen to occur in the line of march.

" On these occasions," thought he, " I have always felt prodigiously thirsty ; beside, I have eaten nothing for four-and-twenty hours since I left Holmes's. Methinks the creature-comfort of a pot of porter would do me as much service as a prayer."

Ere long his attention was caught by a large oblong board, painted of a light blue colour, and swinging vehemently in the breeze which swept the street before him. This sign-board was distinguished from most others by a curious circumstance: we allude to a fine peal of double-bob-majors, which were suspended from its cornice, and which, partaking every vibration of the " *popularis aura*" that regulated the

motion of the wood, proclaimed the gyration, in
notes of the most attractive lusciousness, to the
ear of every passenger in that part of the town.
In letters of brass, solid, clear, and beaming,
appeared the long and famous legend—

Henri Le Grand, his Manufactory:

☞ N.B. **Nothing but works of spirit sold here.**

" Ha !" quoth Smithers, " I have found it
at last. What though my sainted sire ever
preferred the savour of sangaree, natheless may
I in one particular differ from his rubrick, and
yet not merit the reproach of degeneracy.—
Spirit !—yes, spirits it shall be ! I care not
which of the alcoholic streams warms my
stomachic region, provided only the article be
prime of its kind." With such reflections he
opened a glass-paned portal, and found himself
in a moment within a large and spacious building, resounding, in every direction, with the

ever various noises of ever various toil; loud
was the hissing of pens over paper; loud the
snipping of scissors; loud the smack of gum-
rubbing fingers; endless the whiz of revolv-
ing leaves; and yet, clear and high over all
the chaos of sound, rose the shrill commanding
voice of him, who was obviously the master of
the magnificent pile.

" Sir," says Smithers, slowly advancing to
this personage, (a man of gigantic stature, with
a countenance at once majestic and mild, and
an air and presence of the most consummate
elegance)—" Sir, I fear I have made a small
mistake—I thought this was the Cat-and-Bag-
pipes Burlington Street.   But I find that I
have erred in my wanderings, and my feet have
directed me to a region different from that
which I intended to have entered."

Several busy hands were instantly checked in
their career, and sundry eyes, of the most piercing brilliancy, were fixed, as if by the spell of

the basilisk, on the glowing countenance of the intruder.

The master of the manufactory waived his hand, in a condescending and gracious manner, towards our hero, and said—

"Oh, Sir, make no apologies!—I beg you wo'nt—will you please to take a chair, Sir—? Have you seen this here affair—it is a thing much praised, you see—praised in the Papers— yes, the Papers—hum—(a handsome looking volume, evidently wet from the press, which he handed courteously to his guest;) will you be pleased to run your eye over the catalogue? you may find—yes — Sir — perhaps— you understand—Sir—hum!"

Smithers now began to conceive a distant suspicion of the true nature of the mistake of which he had been guilty, and could scarcely suppress a smile, on reflecting over the now apparent facility of his own juvenile credulity; but ere he had time to indulge this natural tendency, he was arrested by the sudden and terrific sternness of air, attitude, and gesture assumed by his collocutor. He was relieved, after a moment's shudder, by perceiving that the coming explosion was destined, not for him, but for some of those persons whose labour had been interrupted by his initiatory address. To interfere would, he felt, be unwise as well as unjust—he expected the burst in silence.

The face of THE MASTER—(such his employés generally called him,) had now assumed a hue more black than purple; and, knitting his massy brows, and grinding his enormous teeth together, and elevating his right arm, with a long and heavy ruler of mahogany in the hand at its extremity, he began to thunder out his indignation in broken phrases, such as these —slapping the ruler on the desk—

" I say, my honest journeymen, what is this ? There's not a man among you who has done a sheet, this blessed day, yet. You idle devils!

but off and away, up and at it; every one
attending to any thing but his work! I
know very well what I'll do, when Saturday the
27th, comes;—confound your lazy fingers! Do
you think I can feed and clothe you, and carry
on my trade, you being as idle as if you were
Spitalfield weavers ? As for you, Sir," said he,
looking at a slim, sallow, pockmarked man,
where is Chapter 28th ? I'll have two per cent.
off you for this, Sir, that's what I will, as sure
as my name's Harry Badger."

He paused for a moment to take breath, and
returned to another victim.

"Shake, shake, aye shake, as you please, you
blubbering booby—I'll shew you what's what.
If the Bell of Midnight is not done by Easter
Sunday, hang me but I'll have you laid as fast
in Whitecross Street, as ever Peter Finnerty
was; and you, Sir," turning to another, "you
passed me off, as materials fit for high life, a
commodity that belonged to a Jew washer-

woman. Dang me, but I could find it in my heart to let them there confounded slinking shoulders feel the taste of ——"

The unfortunate individual was unable to endure this continued appeal to his feelings— he staggered, reeled, and fell senseless on the floor, which being formed of the finest marble, inflicted a severe gash on his forehead, and would in all probability have shattered in pieces any organ of that order, less solidly constructed by the modelling hand of nature. One of the nearest operatives happened fortunately to be of the medical profession, and he hurried, lancet in hand, to bleed him; but his promptness was surpassed by Smithers, who, seizing a large jug which stood on a desk close to him, he bestowed its contents on the prostrate youth. Sable streams deluged his countenance, for our compassionate hero had committed the trifling blunder of mistaking ink for water.

The master displayed, however, a touch of

a feeling mind upon this occasion—for though he was obliged to keep his workmen in order, he was naturally of a kind disposition.

"Get him to bed," said he, "and put some horse turpentine in the cut, and you may give -him some beef-tea with his gruel. You need not come to-morrow to work, my lad."

The grateful looks of the youth as he was borne out, testified his sense of the clemency of his master, and impressed Smithers with a high opinion of the manner in which affairs were carried on in the manufactory. When on the point of resuming the conversation, a neatish little figure strutted into the room, and putting his right hand to his bonnet (which was of blue foolscap), saluted his chief.

"Ay," said our manufacturer, "here's a pattern for you all, you lazy vagabonds! Here comes Reuben Apsley. Here's a man never late at his work—always ready, always steady, as the saying is—always sober; an honest, decent, hardworking tradesman. I wish I had a few more such. What have you brought, Reuben?"

" Three pounds eight ounces of Hebrew work, your honour," said the foreman, for such he was, " which, with what your honour has already, makes five pounds six ounces, the weight of Mr. Wilmot Horton's emigration report. I think a pound or a pound and a half more will do the job entire."

" A better servant never attended master," said the gratified employer.

" It's a pleasure," cries the foreman (for he had tears in his eyes) " to serve such a gemman ; ' good master makes good man'—as old Avon hath it—and though service is no inheritance, yet I d follow your honour ——"

" No matter now," said the master, blushing —" no matter, honest Reuben ; I am obliged to go look after some cattle of the O'Briens and the O'Flaherties, who have emigrated here from Innisfail—I wish to heaven the parliament would do something to keep these people at home—there's nothing but complaints of the mischief they are doing in Lanarkshire, and Lancashire too. As for me, I am literally swarming with them, and my workshop is almost as full of Irish as Buckeridge-street or Bermondsey."

With these words he marched forth with ample steps, flinging his calamanco mantle over his shoulder; and " the halfpence jingled in his pocket" as he crossed the threshold of his far shining resounding portal.

" There you go," said Apsley, " as just a man as ever gave a poor hardworking slave fifteen shillings a week. Sir," said he, turning to Smithers, " you appear to be a stranger——"

Smithers bowed a silent assent.

" In which case," continued the foreman, " you would, mayhap, wish to see our factory."

Smithers bowed again, and the civil operative proceeded to explain the nature of the business.

" Our work," said he, " please your honour,

lies chiefly in three lines : the historical, at the
head of which department I am; the fashionable;
and the Irish.   Of these, in order, which, as a
poet, whose name I do not at this moment recollect, remarks, is Heaven's first law. With which,
then, does your honour wish me to begin ?"

"That is perfectly indifferent to me," said
our hero ;—" but no—on second . thoughts, I
should prefer having the best quality of work
first explained."

"The best quality then," said Apsley, raising
his shoulders, " is the historical ; but it is not
the easiest, because it requires study."

So saying, he went to the private desk, and
took out a greasy, well thumbed MS., like a
house-wife's hereditary cookery-book, and began to read sonorously, the following—

" RECIPE FOR A HISTORICAL NOVEL."

" 'Take Pinnock and Maunder's History of
England, and there find a time when there was a
war or a plot.   Take an ass, and bray him in a

mortar until you make him a hero. Saddle your
ass with panniers, full of the adventures of the
time, and let him work. This is the principal in-
gredient. For a heroine, take a young lady of
mild manners, who is expected to go mad in the
course of the book, and, during her paroxysms,
to quote scraps of verses. To balance her, have
a gay lady, who can talk French, and fall in love
with the hero, who, however, is always to take
the tame one, to the great despair of the other.
This will make some pretty *hors d'œuvres* and
side-dishes, to be served up with love-apple
sauce. The disappointed lady will do for a
devil.

"'The other ingredients are a fool, an old
woman, and a bore. For your fool, take Touch-
stone, and pluck out all his wit, stuffing him instead with scraps of sentences, which are more
consistent with the meaning of the word fool, at
present, they being sheer folly. Your old
woman must be picked out of the filthiest classes

of society, and endowed with the gift of prophecy. She is to make the plot thick. Your
bore must be a punster, or a fellow with a catch-
word—or something of the same kind. Have
him perpetually in the dish.

" ' For style, please your honour,' " he continued, " ' take a book of scandal, or chit-chat
of the day, and steal entire pages from it without mercy, the more the merrier. To make the
conversations consistent, stuff in all the words of
the time, without any regard as to who is to say
them. Make no distinction between the language of a duchess and a coal-heaver. If you
introduce an Irishman, be his rank however
high, or his talents however great, he must
talk redolent of Munster—if a Scotchman, let
him be ever so noble, he must talk the patois of
the gutter-bloods of Edinburgh. A Welchman,
of course, can utter nothing but the gibberish
of Leekland.

" ' Regard not historical facts, for that will only

annoy. Make a man, for instance, see the towers upon Westminster Abbey a hundred years before they were built. So with persons. Describe a good-humoured and good-natured gentleman as a ferocious executioner—degrade a gallant and soldier-like figure into that of a bandy-legged drummer—and so on——

" ' Mix up the hero well with every thing. Make him run *by accident* into the very room where Milton is writing his Paradise Lost; and when you want to empty the contents of your scrap-book, make him fall in, *by accident*, with a man who, *by accident*, knows every body of the time.

" ' If you copy the works of a great man in your line, carefully preserve, with Chinese accuracy, every defect. It is much easier than to copy his beauties; and as you want to make yourself one of the *servum pecus*, the easiest way is best. At first you might think it impossible to copy so closely the works of that great man, and yet

weed out the beauty, the grace, the honour, the
poetry, the gush of genius and of gentleman-
like feeling .that flows over every page, and
leave nothing but the dry bones ; but, ' pa-
tience, perseverance, &c.'—Ah ! God bless your
honour,'" said he, looking up from the book, "them
there are the things for us poor operatives—never
fear, Sir, they will carry a hardworking man over
any obstacle."

Reuben paused for a moment, and resumed
reading in a lower note—in fact, a whisper—

"' Serve up, hot and hot, with puffs ; them you
manufacture yourself, or you hire a regular baker.'
Apropos of that, " said he, ringing a bell, " the
puff-manufacturer has not been here to-day."

A servant man came in on hearing the bell—

" You there," said the foreman, " go, run,
fly to Mr. Blowbladder, and tell him I want
him. I suppose the fellow is drinking somewhere with the printers."

"' And finally,' " continued Reuben—address-

ing our hero from the book—"' and finally, Sir,
get yourself connected with a magazine, which
you supply with light goods—and in return it will
set off your work in its front window ; and—but,
hang me, I should not be telling you every thing.
You may also gratify yourself by using it for
the purpose of saying every thing spiteful against
the works of the great man whose model you
have purloined.'"

Here one of the operatives came up, and with
a reverent air addressed the foreman :

"Musha, then, agra, God be wid you, but
would not yee be after tellin a body whether I
oft for to spell ' of' wid an f or a v ?"

"With a *wee*," said the foreman—"no—stop
—with a *hef*, I believe. Let me see, don't be in
a hurry—but, Sir, do you expect me to be
doing *your* business ? Go look out for it in
Johnson. Do you think I am bound to answer
questions ?"

The abashed Hibernian departed, blushing

with the characteristic modesty of his country, in quest of information. The foreman resumed :—

" A good lad that," said he, " and industrious, but I must keep a strict eye on all these jockies. If I didn't, the master's business would never be done as it ought to be. Some of them —that Jew fellow there, for instance—would sham Abraham."

Mr. Blowbladder here entered, diffusing around him a strong halo of gin.

" I have brought your worship," stammered he, " a pound of puff, which I hope your worship ———"

" Blowbladder," said the foreman, " you are drunk. What do you mean by this, Sir? Your last articles were of the worst quality, and were not at all taking. Sir, it's no use speaking to you—that there one in the Chronicle was as thin as gauze, and did not eat short and crisp. Confound me, Sir, but I only wonder Tom put it in his light column;—for shame, Blowbladder! for shame! for shame!"

Blowbladder listened to this objurgation with infinite composure; and then, with that brazen audacity which the Batavian Bacchus alone can bestow, performed a grin in which two entire lines of tobacco-tainted tusks were revealed to the light of day.

" Do you grin at me, Sir?" shouted Reuben, rubicund with wrath.

" To be sure I do," responded he, squirting a gill of brown juice within half an inch of the other's foot—" To be sure I do; a gentleman of the press is as good any day as a gentleman by act of parliament. Shade of Jim Pirie! is the day come at last when a potter may not grin at his own potsherd without being called to an account for it! You, my good fellow, big a cock as you fancy yourself, are more obliged to me than ever I shall be to you. Have I not puffed your works —— "

" And been paid for it, you rogue—been paid for it handsomely," roared Reuben.

" Handsomely indeed," responded Blow-bladder. " Sir, I despise your dirty penny a line. I get three halfpence for reporting Lord Lansdown's hospitality, or the wonderful cures performed by Mother Burchell's anodyne neck-lace. Did not I make fifteen shillings by de-luding a girl in one of the outlets, through means of a captain of the Guards, who never existed but in my own brain? Did not I fob thirteen and sixpence for finding a man with his throat cut in Hornsey wood a week ago, which likewise was a fanciful effort of my luxuriant imagination? Handsomely, indeed! Why, Sir, Jack Thurtell, my own old friend, honest Jack, put more money in my pocket in one short three months of his life, than all your fry of ———— "

" To cut the matter short," said Reuben——-

" Ay," said Blowbladder, " but I won't let you cut it short. Wasn't it I, that said a cer-

tain person in the North must learn to bear a
rival near his throne, and don't you print it in
your own *ads* to the present day? Wasn't it I
that said you were asked to dine by that same
person, when you were in the North, travelling
for the Master. Wasn't it I that went and
chalked all the walls from Knightsbridge to
Hammersmith, from Mother Redcap's to Jack
Straw's, from the Elephant and Castle to the
Ship at Greenwich, exposing myself to all the
dangers of the treadmill, bidding people ' Buy
REUBEN APSLEY—Cheapest and Best,'
&c. &c. &c.? and now, by the body of Jack
Randall ———— "

Blowbladder had become still more drunk
with his increasing violence, and on using that
tremendous name, he instinctively lifted his arm
to explain to the countenance of Reuben the
nature of the Nonpareil's one-twos; but the
foreman, without further parley, executed a
beautiful backward leap, and cleared in safety

an enormous writing desk, at which fifteen of the fashionable tale-makers were seated.

The whole manufactory was instantly in a state of Babylonian tumult and outcry, and the ever sagacious Smithers made a rush at the door. He attained his object: he was fairly in the street, and at that moment the august Cathedral of Saint Paul's struck NINE.

"Heavens and earth!" cried he, "the hour is come, the glorious, the immortal, the long-expected hour! Breakfast will be ready! Oh! Oh! Oh! Lucy—Lucy will be ready ——!"

He was just about to bound down the street with the speed of an antelope, when he felt some one pulling his button.

"Who are you?" cries Smithers, whom long custom had rendered sensitive to the touch of the bailiff. "What do you want?—Unhand me, caitiff--let me go—I am engaged—don't you hear the summons----?"

"Your honour is abstracted," whispered

Apsley, in an insinuating tone; " I beg pardon if I am troublesome ; but master bade me to be sure not to let your honour quit the shop with-out asking you to give us your adventures since you've been in town. Oh ! do, Sir,—fifty—a hundred—a hundred and fifty—O, Lord, Sir ! you're a knowing one—well, you shall have the cool two hundred—done ?"

" Done," said Smithers ; " done !" and he disappeared amidst the windings of the street.

" Done !" echoed Apsley—" done—done !"

The master manufacturer at that instant re-turned, and with electrical rapidity comprehend-ing the state of affairs, slapped his brawny thigh, and re-echoed " Done, done,

DONE !"

FINIS.

CONCLUSION.

IN A LETTER FROM A FRIEND.

October 20, *A.D.* 2227.

My Dear Sir,

You ask me the fate of some of the persons mentioned in the interesting and agitating narrative of our " historical" friend, (who is now writing for the master a novel of fashionable life, to be called, " Park Lane, or the Annals of Alvanley,") and the dénouement in general of the political adventures of Smithers.   Most of them are matters of historical notoriety.

Truth and justice prevailed for a short time

in the councils of England, and a solemn hearing was given to Smithers, pleading the cause of his murdered father. By the eminent legal abilities and oratory of his two counsel, Messrs. Roaring Rushton, and Trojan Mac Donnell, he partly succeeded, and the Colonial Secretary was destined to die for the atrocious deed. Here, however, occurred a difficulty. *What* Colonial Secretary was to die? the man in office at the time the murder was committed, or the present functionary? And there was a vast contention among the lawyers thereupon.

At last Lord Lyndhurst pronounced judgment.

" It is plain," said that great lawyer, " it must be the present Secretary. A man taking a house, of which the taxes have not been paid, is bound to pay up the arrears of his predecessor. An heir to an estate must answer the liens laid upon it by the former owner. If a person strike a man in the King's presence and

evade for ten years, his hand is cut off at the
end of the period, though it be altered in bone,
muscle and sinew.   So, if A. B. commit a murder and escape for five-and-twenty years, he is
hanged, though (see case of Sir John Cutler,
in Term. Rep. Mart. Scrib.) he is a changed
man in body, and perhaps in mind. But the
principle is laid down distinctly by Lord Coke,
in his Institutes, with the peculiar elegance of
the Latin style of that great man.   ' *Qui capit*,'
says his Lordship, ' *qui capit advantagios, sumit
quoque disadvantagios :*' that is, he who touches
the cash on quarter-day, must submit to be
badgered occasionally. . The judgment of the
Court is, that Lord Bathurst be dismissed from
the bar, and that Mr. Huskisson be hanged.
Fiat instanter.   Look to him, jailor.   *Hoc pro
warranto.*   Hanged by the neck."

Huskisson was taken away in an agony of
terror.   He offered to do anything, to peach, to
turn informer—but this procured him nothing

but an order from Lord Goderich to have him gagged. The anticolonial party, however, were too strong not to make a struggle. When they found it impossible to save their friend, they said it was only fair that they too should have a victim. Conciliation being the order of the day, it was resolved, on the usual principle of the then government, that neither party should have a triumph, and after some deliberation it was determined, that when Mr. Huskisson was hanged, Cæsar should suffer also—for the sake of uniformity. To this arrangement, Cæsar made many objections, but his master convinced him of the absurdity of his scruples, and he submitted.

" The pair was first pilloried at Charing Cross, and then sent to execution. At this time, the old veteran—Mr. Tierney—called at the Treasury to ask for the situation of Prime Minister, which he understood was vacant. He was informed that he was under a mistake, for the office was most ably filled.

" Is there no place vacant, then ?" said the veteran ; " I can do the duties of one or two more beside the mint."

" No—none—" said Lord Goderich : " I mean none that you would take."

" But is there any ?" asked the senior.

" Why, in fact, only one, and that is, the office of hangman, which I know you would not accept."

" The devil I wouldn't," said the veteran— " my dear Lord, it would be an odd thing if I'd refuse a place. No—no—hand me over the patent, and you'll see what a Jack Ketch I'll make. I think it's a business I'll like."

He was of course invested with the collar of the order, and hastened to enter upon the duties of official life at Newgate. Here he found Mr. Huskisson and Cæsar, waiting to receive at his hands the last ceremonies of the law. Huskisson was impenitent, and could not be brought to acknowledge the justice of his sentence. Cæsar, on the contrary, showed a most contrite spirit, and was singing with a harmonious voice at the gallows' foot, the affecting and consolatory psalm of,

> " Adam was de fust man,
> Ebe was anoder,
> Cain was de nex man,
> Him kill him broder."

The ropes, adjusted by the skilful finger of Tierney, soon surrounded their necks; the confining pinion clasped their restricted arms; the snowy cap shrouded their features; Sheriffs Spottiswoode and Stables gave the fatal signal, and in a moment they swung in pendulous death, amid the acclamations of surrounding thousands. Cæsar struggled a little. Huskisson died easily, and instantaneously.

" Well," said the Secretary of the Admiralty,

who attended the execution officially, " I never see Huskisson look so straight and genteel before. By all the crosses in a yard o'check, if you could see how purty you are hanging, Husky, my old sojer, you would try to come to life again, just for the pleasure of seeing how you look when you're dead."

The Dead March in Saul was then played; and the spectators, filled with mournful musings,

" —— with wandering steps, and slow,
    Through Holborn took their melancholy way."

I am, dear Sir,

Faithfully your's,

H. S.

THE END.